Winter

2012 Anthology

Pen Press

First published in Great Britain by Pen Press

All paper used in the printing of this book has been made from wood grown in managed, sustainable forests.

ISBN13: 978-1-78003-533-8

Printed and bound in the UK
Pen Press is an imprint of
Indepenpress Publishing Limited
25 Eastern Place
Brighton
BN2 1GJ

A catalogue record of this book is available from the British Library

Cover design by Jacqueline Abromeit

www.authoressentials.com
0845 519 3977

*'In seed time learn, in harvest teach,
in winter enjoy'*

William Blake

Introduction

At Author Essentials we deal with writers and authors every day. People come to us from all walks of life with books and stories that range from a tentative first step into writing and publishing to downright brilliant books ready for mass market. In winter 2011, we thought it was time we gave something back to the writing community with another of our popular competitions.

The response we again had from writers was fantastic – not just in the number of entries, but also the quality of the writing. As more and more entries came in we found it increasingly hard to narrow it down! It seemed a shame that many of the stories would not find their place in print. And so, we compiled a list of the very best of the entries this year and popped them in this book for the whole world to enjoy.

We contacted Indepenpress – an independent publisher that is passionate about finding new writing talent – as they had been helpful in providing the publishing package prize for our first Flash Fiction competition. This time, we were supplying the prizes, but Indepenpress readily agreed to publish the anthology.

These stories range in genre, length and style. Some are joyous, others bleak. Many were chosen for their creativity and descriptive content, others for the impact they had. Some we loved because of the elaborate styling, some because they were perfectly simplistic. This anthology has it all.

So, dip into this winter wonderland of short stories, when the nights draw in and it's cold outside. We hope this little book warms you inside, and fires your passion for reading and writing.

Contents

Winter

Short Stories

BRENDA AT THE DOORWAY
Martin Towers

It is always winter when I see Brenda in those later days – or, anyway, I suppose it is winter because, looking back, she is always slowly unwinding her scarf from around her neck and taking off her long coat before she sits. I am sat some distance away, glancing at her across the bar, pleased to see her, for some reason I don't really understand – a little intrigued that, once again, she has appeared, flickered in, like a moth in from the darkness, and is there getting herself ready for her night, her full pint of Guinness slowly settling on the table in front of her. And my night, with her arrived, suddenly feeling that little bit different, a different tune beginning to play.

Brenda, you see, had come back into my life after having been a part of it before. We come and go from one another, it seems to me, like ghosts, or like messengers – from somewhere, from something. Brenda, the first time around, had been a part of the village where my days had been centred for many years. She had been one of the characters – albeit a minor one, I had thought – who had inhabited that strange place that had been everything to me for a while.

And then I had been away, for several years; I had been all over, done this and that. When I returned I began to go again to a pub near the village, and straight away, as I walked through the door I would see them – faces from the old place suddenly there and glowing out across at me; or one suddenly there beside me as I stood at the bar, a hand on my shoulder, asking what I was drinking – Steven Murphy, Jimmy McMahon, Little Anna, Boxer. And very quickly too I spotted Brenda, seeing her every night that I was there; the first few times our eyes almost connecting before she pulled them quickly apart, so that I almost wondered if she remembered me at all – while knowing, really, that she did, knowing that it was just her shyness. And then, a little later, I began to pass her at the doorway as I left, as she stood there smoking, as we reconnected, and as she began to say those things to me.

Brenda had always made me wonder. Back there at the village there were much bigger, bolder, noisier acts, headliners if you like – Old Joe of the mad white hair walking in as bold as brass with a whore on his arm after a day in Wetherspoons; Little Jimmy pulling off his shirt and squaring up to Billy, fists raised; Anna shouting, screaming that she'd 'lost every damn thing'. No, Brenda was never the star of the show, more someone up at the back of the stage, in the chorus, who you noticed when your attention drifted away from the one there at the front in the limelight. Because, you felt, there was just something about her, something unusual that you could never quite put your finger on.

Brenda had her chirpy, jaunty little walk; her walk that always looked far too young for her age. It was a girl's walk, but a certain sort of girl's walk, a girl with no wiles about her, who had never swung her hips or glanced back over her shoulder but who jogged jauntily along, chatted with you, smiled, shared cigarettes with you. And Brenda had her toothy smile and her deep, gutsy, smoker's laugh.

I talked to her – about nothing at all – sometimes in those days in the village. 'Hello there!' she would say, always with the exclamation and the chattiness, the chirpiness, but also always the reserve and the shyness. With Brenda there was never anything dark, never any gloom – but there was also always just that hint of mystery around her as she bobbed away up the driveway at the end of her shift, pulling on a cigarette – back with her secrets, I used to feel as I watched her go away.

There was just something about her, Brenda, that I could never quite name or place – until the night at the village when a band came to play, people doing turns, singing old songs badly and dancing together between the candle-lit table tops as if the years had been rolled back and they were young again. And Brenda had got up and stood there with the band behind her and sang – wonderfully, easily, holding the stage and the audience as surely and professionally as she held the microphone, looking for once and for all like someone in their rightful place. So that was it, I thought to myself, that was who Brenda was, a singer, from stages in far back places. That was what it was about Brenda, I thought.

'Brenda! Remember me?' I said as I passed her in the doorway that first time we spoke, the second time around. 'My God!' she said. It was late in the evening and I was leaving with a friend. Brenda pulled her cigarette down form her mouth and gave a skilful mime of surprise. 'My God!' she said again, 'How strange!'. We chatted, briefly, about how long it had been, how we were. I asked her if she lived nearby – she did, she said, on May Lane. And then I said goodbye to her and moved away. 'Bye!' she called after me. She was drunk. 'Please say hello again!' she said. 'Oh do say hello again!'.

And I did – on quite a few occasions, but only ever later in the evening. Earlier, I came to realise, she would still pretend not to notice me – until she had had a few drinks and then I knew that I could raise a hand to her as she passed. She even, sometimes then, came over to stand for a while beside me. And when she did we smiled and stroked each other with kind, meaningless words – how we hoped we didn't get snow, how we'd seen so and so from the village days, how it was a hard life, how you had to struggle on...

And then those other times at the doorway – always, it seemed, when I was with someone and unable to stop. But I would always greet her as I passed her stood there at the edge of the night, asking her if she was OK. And it was then that she surprised me. 'I'm not sure actually!', I heard her say, quite loudly after me. Something unexpected, something unknown and serious perhaps but still delivered with that same jauntiness, the exclamation. Her words trailing after me into the frosty night, taking root and slowing, just a little, my stride. And then another time, a few weeks later when I passed her again, again asking her if she was ok. 'I hope so!' she called this time, the last time I spoke to her.

A few weeks later the snow that me and Brenda hoped wouldn't come had fallen and I sat on the bus going down May Lane on my way into town. Brenda had come to inhabit those rides for me – because I now knew that I would, at some point, be passing her home. The bus came to a halt and I looked and saw that there was an ambulance stopped at the roadside ahead of us. The bus pulled out and around it, and as we moved on I looked out of the window just as the door to a little terrace opened and the paramedic began to wheel Brenda up the garden path. Brenda sitting there with the white blanket around her up to her chin and a belt around her. I saw her only for an instant but could see her head turned up and around to say something to the man who pushed her. Her wonky teeth bared in a nervous grin. Her head shaking from side to side a little in that way she had. She would, I knew, be making some bright, jokey remark – even then. 'This doesn't look too promising!' I could imagine her saying, or something similar – something that would seem like a line from a happy song that you could tap your feet to as she sang the words.

I went away again for a while soon after that. When I returned, while I hoped each time the door of the pub opened it would be Brenda coming through, somehow, deep down, I knew that it wouldn't be. One afternoon when I was there, the place more or less empty, Steven Murphy came and sat with me. We talked of this and that, who we'd seen. Steve made a careful remark about me having been away, nothing prying, nothing pressing, just a mention of it with his face turned away as he raised his glass to his lips, to give me the option, I knew, of leaving it if I wanted to, and I just said how cold it was there, how cold it had been

So we spoke on about other things, he told me some stuff about the building days, about his son, and then, when that had all dried up I said to him that I hadn't seen old Brenda for a while and how the last time I'd seen her I'd seen her being taken off in an ambulance. And Steve said then that Brenda had died two months before.

Steve said that a few of them had been to the funeral She was a nice old thing he said. And we started to talk about her a bit more. I said how she'd always puzzled me, in a way. I said to Steve that there's not many women you see walking into a pub on their own in the way she did; I said there's not many of them just sit down with a pint of Guinness there, or have a wander around and see who they can have a chat, a drink with. Steve said I was right, I wasn't wrong – she was unusual in that way, old Brenda. He said did I know about her singing? And I said I didn't, not really, only that I had been there that night at the village when she'd sung with the band. And Steve said that, apparently, she'd used to sing for a living, way back. He said he'd heard that years ago her and some bloke used to have an act that toured the seaside theatres. He said that he supposed they'd been down the list, supporting, so to speak, but yes, she'd spent years at it so they say.

And then Steve leant forward a bit and touched my arm and looked to both sides and he dropped his voice and said he'd heard this other thing about her, that, when she was young, some big-time singer who was top of the bill on one of these tours had knocked her up and she'd had to give the kid away. Steve looking down and to one side and saying how he couldn't remember the fecking fella's name. But then saying did I remember a song from when I was a kid called Wooden Heart? 'Who did that one now?' he said. And I couldn't remember – even though I remembered the song.

I certainly remembered the song. The folks who had brought me up had it. They used to play their records on their little record player on a Sunday morning when they'd had a few drinks and were

7

getting the table ready for dinner. The early nineteen sixties. The one time when I'd overheard them say the thing they'd said about that song, and about me.

I was coming rushing in from the back garden, my hands frozen from playing in the snow. I heard the song as I burst in through the back door and then I heard the woman, just as she was finishing saying to the old fella that he shouldn't play this one while he, while I, I knew she meant, was about. Her voice low, hushed and somehow urgent. But I'd heard her. 'Don't be so daft woman!' the old fella had said.

And I had always remembered that, those few words – had always wanted to know what it was they could possibly mean. Sometimes when I was alone in the house I played the record and sat there listening, wondering; wondering on inside myself as the years went by until it just became a thing in my life – a thing in its worn, fusty sleeve, filed away, forgotten but still there. Because, whatever they were, they had buried themselves inside me, the words had, the song had, had somehow slowed forever that run in from the garden and the snow, my 'brothers' still out there behind me, together and shouting.

And here, there, now, as I sat with Steve, as we carried on with our talk and our drinks I knew inside myself that my life had probably changed again – with another few words, with what Steve had just said. And I wanted to finish my drink and go, get outside – to another answer, another option, that I knew would be out there waiting for me and would be just as big and full and real as I ever wanted to make it.

I see Brenda as she unwinds that long scarf from her neck, as she takes off her winter coat and sits, with the Guinness settling there before her – the long sandy night-storm of it that settles, at last, into a thick, dense, white-capped blackness. Seeing her clearly now – Brenda. Seeing that, once upon a time, she had been touched, by glamour, with all its sharp pressed trousers and shiny Chelsea boots; that she had spent her day, her hour, her fifteen minutes with it and then had it stay on with her for the rest of her life – even as she vacuumed and cleaned – stayed there deep inside like a drag on a long cool cigarette as she walked on and up and away.

I went to her grave once, later – walked there and stood for a while beside her. A wooden cross with just her name on it; a family a few graves up – a chap and his teenage daughter stood waiting while the woman bent and tended a parent's grave; a song thrush singing from a winter tree; a long slow stillness all around; and Brenda gone.

COLOUR IN THE WHITE
Sharon Boyle

"Tomorrow."

The old man, hairpin-bent and dusty, delivered his word, turned, and shuffled back through the gate. The cloths around his feet caught and scuffed the unevenness of the floor.

Gail shivered despite the filthy duvet happed round her body. It must be around eleven at night, but as watches refused to work, she could only guess.

And so tomorrow it would happen. There was nothing to do but wait. All the speeches had been spoken and parcelled up in the camp records, and any further appeals may as well be shouted up to the drained skies.

She had asked for magazines, a cherished commodity and great bartering tool. And they surprised her by relenting and tossing one through; Guide to the Best Electrical Goods. She had hoped for a travel or cookery brochure or even one on fashion, but supposed they had to get in their last dig. Her gloved fingers casually flicked through pages of televisions and dishwashers, but then stopped and hovered over a photograph showing an overly grinning man standing behind a tomato red lawnmower. Gail absorbed the green grass; the man's healthy build; his patch-free and ironed clothes, but most of all, the strong yellow tinge of the sun. The colours seemed violent and the whole page glowed. Gail salivated, her memory trying to tease out the sensation of thick, bold rays on bare flesh.

A cough pierced her daze. Preacher Martin was hanging outside the makeshift cell, peering through the slats.

"Do you wish company, Mrs Wilson?" He used her surname to signal formality.

"Yes. Thank you," she granted, thinking, 'I do want company. I want the company of this vigorous man on paper who doesn't have a beard to keep out the cold and I want to lie on grass that is obscenely green and soak up the lemon rays of a proper, working sun.'

But she knew that in real time Magazine Man's skin had probably been flailed by the wind and his bones eroded by ice. Those in the cities and towns had been the first to fall to disease, hunger, murder and madness. It's what the newscasters on television and radio had screamed before all communication lines were crisped to frosty extinction.

She would have to make do with this homespun preacher. A product of the many zealous men who had sprung forth like bristling weeds and forced themselves up the levels of newly tiered populations. Folks started to realise there would be no deliverance from the constant winter; that the bludgeoning winds and splintering ice were here to stay. They turned scared and this new class of holy do-gooders out vied one another with their monologues of spit and fire. Former heathens clung to the Bible like a lifebelt and soaked up the preachers' words.

"Are you repenting or not?" Preacher Martin was not one for cordiality. Never had been, even when he lived three doors away from her in their neat village. He would merely nod his head in a good morning or give a nugatory smile at her polite enquiry after his wife, Angela. Angela, who had experienced life from a king-sized bed after a long term fight with a sputtering heart. She had been one of the first in their village to be felled by the change in climate, for the sick, and those at either end of the mortal spectrum, had perished in those early lung-gasping months. Gail wondered if Angela's quick death had kick started Martin's switch in job from accountant to self-satisfied, self-appointed preacher.

"I shall not repent because he gave his permission," Gail insisted, again. They had refused to accept this. They had demanded her contrition; wanted an apology; for her to scream out that she had sinned like she was some medieval witch threatened with a drowning.

Preacher Martin's thick lips flat-lined in annoyance. "Your sin will be rightfully punished.

You know we cannot countenance such behaviour. If you repent you may yet save your soul."

"I have done nothing wrong." Gail gave each word its own sentence. Then she sighed, "I will not repent, but I do ask that you stay with me till morning."

Preacher Martin nodded. Their number was small now; only a handful left from the original two thousand odd and he had to admit he would miss her vibrancy. In these brutal times, the gift of optimism was precious, and Gail Wilson had risen above the soul-sucking white monotony of their world to display a generosity that still allowed her to laugh or let go a snippet of song. Even although the sin of eating her husband's flesh was sickening, he would agree to pray for her.

"Is there anyone else you wish to speak to?" he enquired.

"Is that a joke?" she squinted at her old neighbour, smiling with a crooked lip; a slight flirt which fell like glass on concrete.

Nobody would speak to her, even though, she thought bitterly, they would have done the same.

She thought back to Colin's feverish pleas and to the will he had written with sore, blackened hands: *I hereby give permission for my wife, Gail Wilson, to eat my flesh after my death. I am resolute on this and whole heartedly wish this to be so, her loving husband, Colin Wilson.*

The butchered body of her husband, once muscle-thick and painted with serpents, had been found by a keen nosed neighbour under a blanket of rats in the basement. A wave of horror instantly spooled around the camp. It had come to this.

The preacher spoke. "The leaders are scared that others will copy, eat their loved ones; perhaps even resort to murder to get at flesh."

"I understand, and I think you are right. I think that will happen." She studied his faced, hollowed by hunger and need. She had been demented when she sliced at Colin's legs and arms. Her stomach had crunched and twisted with hunger spasms that surmounted any disgust. How long would Preacher Martin and the rest of them last on rats?

Long strips of a beaten sun quavered through the cracks in the canvas. It would be light for only a few hours.

"It's time, now," stated Preacher Martin and he held out his hand for hers. He led her from the cell and on through the slipshod camp; flimsy tents puffing in the breeze and thin coils of smoke rising from weedy fires that failed to heat anyone. The endless moving around to elude the wilder winds was a constant in their lives.

"Ah, the camp leaders have rounded up a crowd to see off the sinner, I see." Preacher Martin did not reply and Gail felt resentment sluice through her at the camp's cheap morality for not killing her, but allowing instead, Nature to do the job.

"If you manage to reach another camp then that is God's will and you are spared." This was spoken at her trial, a righteous speech that assuaged their guilt.

Preacher Martin reached the camp threshold and stopped. Gail did not look at any face, did not heed their silent staring. She peered out to the sheeted landscape: treeless, flat and white.

Preacher Martin let go her hand and she started to walk, away from them all, without a hint of panic or shame. Her back remained straight and her head up, for she was not witnessing the white emptiness that cowed the rest of them. Just before the grey horizon she could see, plainly and brilliantly, the glad grin of a man with bare arms. He was working on a tomato red lawnmower, fixing some mechanism gone haywire. He wiped a strong arm across his forehead and she saw it was tattooed with coiling snakes. Then he stopped and turned her way, raising his arm in a wave, his body and mind happy under the thick, furred rays of a proper, working sun.

LEOPARDS OF THE SNOW
Steve Wade

Higher than all the surrounding mountains, Mount Snowtopia stretched into the clouds. The people who lived on the mountain were called Snowtopians. Everything in their mountain village was made of snow and ice. They lived in houses carved from great blocks of frozen water, which were plastered daily by heavy snowfalls. They sat in chairs and slept in beds hand-crafted from packed snow. For breakfast they crunched their frosty-coated cereals out of crystal bowls so cold you had to wear thick gloves to prevent your hands from freezing.

Direct sunlight on the mountain was banned, and no artificial heat was allowed. Any rise in temperature, Snowtopia's scientists predicted, and the school, the church, the shops and the houses, all constructed from snow and ice, would melt. Consequently, all year round the mountain had one season only: winter.

To survive the low temperatures, the Snowtopians wore furry coats and hats woven from the wool of mountain sheep imported from the people who lived in the lower hills. Permanent winter on the mountain meant that no vegetation grew, and with no plants on which to feed, wild animals stayed away. Well, all except one creature: Ookpik, Grandfather Frost's pet snowy owl. As his top scout, Grandfather Frost sent the owl on regular visits to the mountain to ensure all remained stable on Snowtopia.

Only one month to the Yuletide celebrations now and the snow-covered mountain looked like an elaborately decorated Christmas cake. Perched on the very top of the mountain, the ice palace hotel sparkled beneath the moonlight. The villagers depended on the visiting tourists, their income and the industry brought in by the hotel. But this year was the coldest anyone could remember. And, as no fires were permitted on Snowtopia, the weavers and tailors busied themselves with orders for clothes with thicker lining and extra wool.

For the mountain villagers, accustomed to extreme cold, the new woolly garments kept them almost as warm as snow leopards adapted to sheltering in caves during a fierce blizzard. Not so the tourists. The hotel catered for over five hundred visitors but with less than thirty days to Christmas, there were nine guests made up of one family and a newlywed couple. And both parties had informed Mikhail Alexandrov, the hotel owner, of their intentions to leave as soon as the latest cold spell lifted and a sled and dogs could be used to whisk them safely down the treacherous mountain path.

Like the hoary breath that had turned the snowfall on the mountain to a treacherous shroud of ice, panic gripped the mountain people, turning, it seemed, even their thoughts to frozen and impenetrable fear. People regarded each other through eyes that didn't appear to register. They listened with ears that couldn't hear beyond their own sense of impending dread. Only one man, the owner of the ice hotel, remained calm. Time to call a meeting, he decided.

Dressed in their extra warm coats, capes and hats, the Snowtopians arrived to the hotel meeting room. Those living close to the hotel trudged through the heavy snow on snowshoes; some on snowmobiles, while others came on sleds pulled by anxious huskies that yipped and yapped. Little conversation did they exchange together beyond how relaxed Mikhail Alexandrov looked. And, indeed, nobody could recall the hotel owner ever looking any way other than at ease with himself and the world in all the years they had known him.

The murmurs petered out when Mikhail climbed the steps to the stage and stood before a microphone.

Without introduction or explanation, he opened with just three words: "The snow leopard," he said, paused, smiled, stepped back from the microphone and let his eyes wander around the puzzled crowd. He then stepped forward. "The snow leopard is the solution to our problem, my friends."

The Snowtopians turned to each other, shook their heads and frowned. "His brain has seized up," said a mechanic who specialised in snowmobiles.

The snow-carpenter agreed. "Mikhail's head has finally turned to sawdust slush," he said.

Before he went on to give them a short lecture on the snow leopard, the hotel owner drew his audience's attention to a very special guest who had just flown in from the faraway and ancient woodland of Veliky Ustyung: Ookpik, Grandfather Frost's pet snowy owl.

The crowd turned round to see Ookpik perched high up on the ceiling's chandelier made from a thousand diamond-shaped ice-cubes. Mikhail Alexandrov invited Ookpik to join him on stage.

"Hooo-uh, hooo-uh," Ookpik said, left his perch and sailed on silent wings over the heads of the Snowtopians and came to rest on a frozen tree-stump placed for that purpose next to Mikhail Alexandrov's lectern.

The crowd applauded.

Now that he had their full attention, Mikhail Alexandrov told them of his ingenious plan to bring back the tourists to Snowtopia. The leopard, he explained, was perfectly adapted to a freezing mountainous environment, exactly like the conditions on Snowtopia. The animal's body was stocky and its fur dense, its feet wide to distribute body weight on soft snow, and, most importantly, the cat's tail was so round and thick, the leopard used it like a blanket to keep its face warm while it slept during particularly bad weather.

By the looks on some of the faces, Mikhail Alexandrov believed his plan already beginning to stick and whiten, spreading like fallen snow.

"It takes about six snow leopard skins to make a fur coat," he said.

Around the hall the crowd exchanged looks of horror. They nonetheless applauded. For everyone knew how ruthless Mikhail Alexandrov could be in business, but the idea of killing the snow leopards was lunacy.

A wink from Ookpik in their direction, however, reassured them that Grandfather Frost would soon be aware of their troubles.

For now they didn't dare show any disapproval. The livelihood of every man and woman on Snowtopia depended on Mikhail Alexandrov and his ice palace hotel. In the past a few Snowtopian's had disagreed with him about the permanent ban on sunshine. Without discussion, Mikhail Alexandrov had banished these men to the lower hills.

So, for their future's sake, the audience cheered, whooped and clapped their hands.

Mikhail nodded. "Yes," he said. "You understand me. We can offer our guests coats, hats and moccasins fashioned from the animal whose fur is thick enough to live all-year round with Grandfather Frost, if he so decided." He shifted his attention to Ookpik beside him and raised his eyebrows. Ookpik blinked his huge yellow eyes, but showed no emotion.

One of the tailors in the centre of the crowd, a normally quiet man, put up his hand. His bloated face seemed ready to implode.

"Yes sir," Mikhail said.

"The tails," he said. "The tails will make wonderful scarves." The tailor had no intention of fashioning scarves from the animal's tails. He just wanted to please the hotel owner.

"Exactly," Mikhail said. "We're driving in the same blizzard you and I."

Not used to compliments, the tailor chuckled, pressed his hand to his mouth, and glanced about for further approval.

Mikhail Alexandrov then explained that he had learned from a guest one time that there was around three and a half thousand snow leopards left in the world – a sufficient number to fashion more than five hundred coats and other garments: plenty for his hotel guests. Getting hold of these leopard skins, he said, would be difficult. For one thing, there were no guns in Snowtopia. Without creatures to hunt, weapons were unnecessary. Besides, a single rifle report was likely to start an avalanche. So all weapons, like the sun, were banned.

He had considered purchasing the hunting equipment from the towns and villages in the lower mountains. But the Snowtopians were a private people and, beyond trading with outsiders and catering for their visitors, they kept their affairs to themselves as best they could. No, he had an alternative plan: the job of tracking down and

21

capturing alive the snow leopards would be given to the husky trainers and handlers. The handlers were the only Snowtopians ever to move through the world outside Snowtopia. A necessity when they travelled to collect their dogs. These men were experienced in the ways of animals. They lived with them, knew their dietary and physical requirements. They understood them. And if they could learn the ways of one creature, they could learn and master the ways of another.

Like everybody else, the dog trainers and handlers valued their jobs, and so agreed to carry out the hotel owner's plan. Besides, as soon as Grandfather Frost learned from Ookpik Mikhail Alexandrov's crazy plan to turn the snow leopards into fur coats, no harm could surely come to these elusive creatures.

Mikhail Alexandrov's theory about the dog handlers and keepers' knowledge of animals proved right. Within a few weeks, they returned from far-flung places like China, Afghanistan, Mongolia, Nepal and India, their sleds crammed with nearly three thousand snow leopards thrust up like deer with ropes made from sheep's wool around their legs.

The meeting room in the ice palace they used as a temporary communal cage to await the arrival of the butcher from the lower mountains. No choice had Mikhail Alexandrov at this stage except to let an outsider know about the – up till now – very secret project. Off he sent by moonlight a dog musher, his sled and team for the lower hills, ensuring that he keep secret from the butcher the need for his services until his arrival in Snowtopia.

On his journey downhill and across the jagged hills and open tundra, the musher in his loneliness and guilt cried out for Grandfather Frost's help.

From their beds of snow in their icehouses, the Snowtopians could hear the wails and growls made by three thousand snow leopards coming from the ice palace. They too, unable to sleep, awaited Grandfather Frost's arrival. Filled with doubt, they imagined terrible possibilities: maybe Ookpik got caught up in a snowstorm and never made it home to VelikyUstyung. What if Grandfather Frost's beautiful daughter the Snow Maiden was ill and he had to stay by her bedside? And a million other tragedies they imagined through the long, dark night.

Just before dawn something strange began to happen. The dry coldness of their beds was replaced by a warming wetness; and from the ceilings fell droplets, at first intermittently and then steadily. Everything was melting. There followed shouts and cries around the mountain as people called out to neighbours their horror at the brightening mountains below them. Overnight the snow had completely melted. The lower mountains appeared as they did in springtime: lush and green.

Baying dogs turned the Snowtopians attention to the dog handler and the butcher arriving at a slow pace through slushy snow.

Mikhail Alexandrov quickly informed the butcher as to why he had been summoned. But asked him even more speedily for his ideas on this strange phenomenon.

The butcher shook his jowly face. "Oh my word," he said. "You've ruined us all. Oh my word."

The hotel owner told the butcher to calm down, and granted him that he would accept responsibility for whatever harm he may have caused, but what exactly had he ruined and how?

"Winter," the butcher said. "With most of the snow leopards removed from the mountains, Winter has been fooled. He believes it time for him to go on his holidays and has left to join his friend Autumn elsewhere in the world."

But how could that be? Grandfather Frost controlled the seasons. The consequences, however, for Mikhail Alexandrov, were as stark as a whiteout. Springtime, confused too, seemed to have got excited and travelled on up in to Snowtopia where she must have heard the miaows, hisses and growls of the snow leopards.

To all listening to the exchange between the hotel owner and the butcher, a realisation, like the North Wind's breath laced with icicles, swept over them. Every head twisted towards the mountaintop and the collapsing ice palace, followed by three thousand snow leopards charging and bounding down the mountain.

Men, women, children and dogs, shouted, screamed, yelped and scattered while the leap of leopards sprinted, slipped and slid by them back to the freedom of their own lands.

When all had finally settled down, they watched a large figure and a smaller one approaching from the ruined ice palace: Grandfather Frost and his daughter the Snow Maiden. Dressed in his red and gold heel-length fur coat, Grandfather Frost stepped back to allow his daughter arrive before him.

"Happy Christmas," she said to Mikhail Alexandrov, and held out to him something small and white.

Mikhail accepted the gift.

Everybody gasped at the thing given Mikhail by the girl.

Never had they seen anything so wondrous. Such perfection. Like a snowflake before it came to rest and bled into a thousand others, but what was it?

"It's a snowdrop," the Snow Maiden said. "I guess it's been sleeping under the snow forever, just waiting to wake up."

Mikhail Alexandrov let his head droop into his own chest. "I'm so sorry," he said to Grandfather Frost. "My need to save the hotel and the livelihood of all of Snowtopia left me snow-blind to the rights of other creatures."

Grandfather Frost touched Mikhail's shoulder with his magical staff. "There are those who make mistakes and learn nothing," he said. "You have learned well. Now, come. It's Christmas. I have a gift for you and your people."

A piercing whistle screeched from the air, pulling the Snowtopians' gaze skyward.

"An eagle," Grandfather Frost offered without being asked. Ookpik, on his shoulder crouched and clacked his beak as a warning to the eagle.

Hearing the eagle's cry, the Sun stirred and pushed aside the grey clouds.

The rays from the Sun on the people's raised faces caressed like a mother's touch.

By nightfall Winter, a little embarrassed at being duped by Grandfather Frost, had returned to Snowtopia. As he passed the retreating Springtime, both seasons were too ashamed to acknowledge the other with even a glance.

But, following Grandfather Frost and the Snow Maiden, Mikhail Alexandrov and the mountain people were already nearing the lower hills to live a new life and celebrate their first Christmas where the Sun shone, flowers bloomed, the eagle soared, and where the snow leopard, wearing his beautiful coat, roamed free and let the seasons know their time to shine.

THE LIVING DOLL
Michael Brookes

Mary or Rosie, as she was now called, looked out from her cramped, lonely bedroom onto the desolate street below. Today was her eighth birthday and this birthday would be no different from all her others. She should have been waiting with impatient excitement for her little friends to arrive for her disco birthday party. She should have been playing with her birthday presents. She should have been trying to blow up another balloon. She should have been watching her mom lay the table, placing eight candles on the 'funky girl' birthday cake. Today should have been the second happiest day of Rosie's year. But it wasn't. There were no friends, no party, no balloons, no cake and no presents. Rosie had never celebrated a single birthday.

'If your sister can't have a birthday party then why should you? I never want you to forget that Rosie.' Debbie was a harsh mother and would repeat this every year, yet Rosie still loved her. After being abandoned at the hospital as a baby, Debbie was the only 'mom' Rosie had ever known. She had no idea what it truly felt like to be loved.

The 'sister' Debbie was referring to was her own biological child, who had also been called Rosie and who was now buried in the cemetery directly opposite the house. A house Debbie and her husband Simon had moved into shortly after the new born babies' funeral.

Simon would regularly listen to Debbie wallow in her own self-pity. Phrases would be thrown about on a day to day basis such as 'it's so hard for me' and 'nobody understands'. But all he did was listen. All it would have taken was a few words to the adoption agency or their social worker and maybe he could have helped his sad excuse for a family. Instead, whenever they got a check-up call Debbie would manage to deliberately deceive them, creating a loving family environment and making a fuss of Rosie. At school, Rosie's teachers saw a bubbly little girl with long dark hair and sparkling eyes. Little did they know that Rosie was only happy here because she had friends. At school she could play and learn, it was worlds away from the dullness and bleakness of her bedroom.

Rosie was still looking out of her bedroom window when she saw Debbie crossing the road, carrying a small posy of flowers to her daughter's grave. Lying back on her bed Rosie's thoughts turned to her next birthday,

'If I'm good all year then Mommy will let me have a party next year' Already Rosie started making plans in her head of who she would invite but Debbie's thoughts were now only for herself. Over the years she had gradually become resentful and bitter, especially towards anyone who was eight years old and still alive.

For most children, the best time of year is Christmas. For Rosie, this Christmas was going to be one to remember. For the first time she was going to see Santa Claus. Simon had finally given into his conscience and decided to do something decent for the little girl, even though it would infuriate his wife.

'What do you want for Christmas?' the jolly Santa asked from behind his false white beard.

Innocent little Rosie was perched on Santa's knee, she looked up at the red, chubby face and replied,

'For my mommy and daddy to love me.'

Taken by surprise and a little embarrassed the Santa glanced at Simon, who was equally embarrassed but sadly, not surprised.

'I'm sure they already do, I meant what present do you want?'

'I would really like to be a Brownie.'

'I didn't mean that either!' The Santa man laughed, but Rosie had already started reciting the Brownie promise.

'I promise that I will do my best to…'

'Well there you are then!' beamed Santa. 'You're already a Brownie.'

The next day was the yearly visit from the adoption agency. Debbie carried out a plate of homemade biscuits whilst Rosie eagerly explained to the social worker about how she was now a Brownie.

'That's lovely!' The social worker wrote it down in her report whilst Debbie gave Rosie a false smile,

'Aren't you a lucky girl.'

Christmas Eve soon approached and Simon's guilt about his adopted daughter festered. With a lot of courage (and a lot of practicing in front of the mirror) he couldn't help but finally tell his selfish wife how he felt,

'We've been terrible parents.'

'Rubbish.' Debbie's expression was as icy as the snow on the pavements outside and her tone was even colder. 'How many mothers have had to go through the trauma that I have? Not many. How DARE you question my parenting skills with what I've been through.'

For once in their entire marriage Simon was going to be assertive. This woman who he had once loved now infuriated him; grief had turned her into a human monster. He spoke quietly, but his tone showed the rage that was bubbling up inside him.

'We have both been through a lot. But so has Rosie. We have failed to be proper parents to that little girl upstairs, I could have cried last week hearing her tell Santa that all she wanted was for her parents to love her. Why would she say that?'

Debbie went to answer, she planned to say something like, 'She's spoiled, she wants more than we can give her.' But Simon didn't give her the chance.

'No, don't answer. Don't even try to answer. We are no better than her real parents, they abandoned her and so have we. I am not going to ignore my daughter's needs anymore! This year I have actually bought her a Christmas present. It's a living doll' Taking a deep breath he pointed to large box that was wrapped in snowman paper underneath the tree, the only present which was addressed to Rosie.

Debbie's blood suddenly grew a lot warmer, her rage was almost visible, she clenched her fists as she searched for her release, which turned out to be a flower filled, glass vase given to them by Simon's mother. The vase crashed into the eight foot Christmas tree in the corner of the room and shattered into hundreds of pieces, flowers and water were dispersed amongst the shiny baubles and flashing fairy lights.

'I always knew you didn't love me or MY Rosie!' the words slithered from between her teeth as she maintained a hateful expression.

Without giving him chance to answer, she attacked him. With flailing fists she swung pathetic punches at him. At first he just protected himself, easily blocking the volley of feeble, girlie hits, but as the frenzy continued he was forced to act, catching both her hands and holding her at arm's length.

'I do love you!' he pleaded, but she spat at him.

It was only a gentle push backwards but she made a meal of it, diving straight into the middle of the tree. Clattering into the baubles, stripping them from the branches as she grabbed hold, steering herself towards the oblong, snowman box and deliberately crushing it under her own body weight.

Simon's shoulders dropped as did his heart, this one single action had finally proved to him that she was right. He didn't love her anymore. He couldn't even remember when he last had.

'I pity you; what's more I pity me. I just hope that Rosie can forgive us, and for your information, you selfish, inconsiderate bitch, I mean both Rosies because I bet our daughter in heaven has been watching us in shame.' Simon stormed out, slamming the front door behind him.

Weeping silently into her hands, Rosie sat at the top of the stairs. Not even Santa could make them love her now.

Rosie didn't hear her mom crying in the bedroom next door, nor did she hear her father return in the early hours of the morning. Drunk, Simon stumbled into the living room, swaying from side to side, closing one eye as he focused on the floored Christmas tree. He could just make out the fairy lights, which were still blinking. Simon had been tipsy once before but he had never been drunk. He made several attempts to grab one of the blurred branches before pulling the tree back upright. He tried to replace the fallen lights that were still socked with water from the smashed vase.

Suddenly, a two hundred and forty volt shot into his body. For a moment he wondered why he was now sitting on the floor on the other side of the darkened room. Eventually through his drunken stupor he was able to work out what had happened.

'Bugger!' he cursed. He carried on cursing whilst he searched the kitchen cupboards (and the fridge) for the torch.

'Little torchy, where are you? Ah, there you are!'

Click, click, click…

'Oh poor little broken torchy, now where's that bloody candle?'

He soon gave up trying to work out which fuse had blown and staggered back into the lounge where he watched, by candlelight, the Christmas tree spin round and round.

'I do feel sick,' he slurred, and he was. He threw up all over the tree, then smiling a drunken smile his head gently rocked in rhythm with the spinning tree and he passed out, dropping the burning candle into a pile of Christmas gifts.

The fire took hold quickly, flames spread into the damp and broken branches of the eight-foot spruce. Thick smoke filled the room, spilling out into the hallway, swirling up the stairwell towards the smoke detector that failed to activate and warn Debbie of the impending danger. The same smoke detector that earlier in the day had the battery removed by Simon for use in the 'Living Doll' Christmas present, which was slowly melting beneath the tree.

Debbie woke with a start, the room lit only by the amber glow of a streetlamp outside her bedroom window, lifting her head slightly she smelled the air, immediately recognising the smell of her greatest fear.

'Rosie!' she screamed. Still half asleep she rolled off the bed and snatched open the bedroom door, like the wall of a dam the door had been holding back the ever-growing mass of thick, deadly, black smoke. In an instant the air was sucked from the room, whistling past her legs, drawn down the stairway towards the hungry flames. In the same moment a tidal wave of dark, dense smoke rushed into the room, crashing over her, plunging her into absolute darkness. Debbie raised both her arms as if to defend herself and took a sharp and lethal intake of breath. The noxious gas filled her lungs as she began to drown in the sea of smoke. After only a few steps forward she collapsed to her knees.

'Rosie,' she choked, coughing and heaving.

'Get out, Get out.' Blindly she still crawled forward, desperately searching for Rosie's door. The hot smoke was scorching her throat and burning her lungs, with her eyes streaming she slowly sank to the floor. Softly resting her head on the carpet she spoke her last words,

'Forgive me...Rosie...Please forgive me...'

Behind the closed door the young girl was frozen with fear, curled up in the corner of her room, hot tears rolling from her terrified eyes, she didn't even hear her mom's final words.

'Mom?...Dad?' she whispered, too afraid to call out.

A passer-by raised the alarm.

Fire fighters were on the scene within two minutes; the fire was out in five.

The official report into the cause of the fire was an electrical fault in the Christmas tree lights. The fire investigator stated that a properly maintained smoke detector could have saved the adults lives.

Simon's partially burnt body was recovered from the settee in the living room. Debbie died of smoke inhalation; her body was recovered on the landing outside Rosie's closed bedroom door. Rosie was rescued alive and uninjured; though some believe she will never truly recover.

Six years later and in a box under her bed Rosie still keeps her one treasured memory of her parents, a lightly melted and lightly charred living doll.

A NIGHT IN WINTER
S D West

Alice was afraid it would be dark before she arrived at the cottage. She had been delayed leaving London and now as she drove down the motorway to Sussex the wan light of a mid-December afternoon was already fading. She had booked the weekend break at short notice – two nights at the cottage before spending Sunday with an old friend near Hastings.

The description and picture on the agent's website promised a relaxing break in a traditional cottage nestling in a fold of the Downs, the end house of a small hamlet strung out along a narrow, unmade lane. At last, Alice could unwind after several months without any proper breaks from work.

As dusk fell she stopped in the centre of the village where she was to collect the key from the caretaker. "I've aired the house and put on the electric heating," said the caretaker, a thin grey-haired woman wearing corduroy trousers and a sleeveless quilted jerkin over a thick brown jumper, "but you will also find a supply of logs for the fireplace just by the back door."

Alice took the key and smiled. "Thanks, it will be nice to have a real fire in the evenings. By the way, is there a shop in the village?"

The woman pointed further down the street. "Only the post office and store, just further down – it'll be shut now but you can get newspapers there in the morning."

Alice would have liked to ask more about the village and the history of the cottage, but there was something in the woman's manner that made her hesitate. She seemed polite, but not inclined to conversation. Possibly she had been inconvenienced by Alice's late arrival.

After thanking her again, Alice climbed back into the car and drove the mile and a half to the hamlet, along the lane sunken between tall hedgerows.

She reached the cottage shortly after half past four. It was now dark but a lamp switched on as she drew up, the sensor reacting to the car as it passed, and the circle of light was just enough for her to tell that everything was exactly as she had imagined – there was dark green ivy climbing to the eaves at one end and she could dimly make out a climbing rose on the front wall, with the last few yellowed leaves twisting gently from its stems.

She followed the narrow brick path that wound past the front windows round to the side door and let herself in. The door led into a small lobby beyond which was the kitchen. To the right, at the far end of the kitchen was a further door to the sitting room. She unpacked the food, some wine, walking boots and the change of clothes she had brought. "I shall feel quite at home here," she thought, deciding to light the fire. "It will be very cosy" and she looked forward to catching the rich scent of wood smoke and seeing the flames flickering up at the mellow bricks inside the inglenook.

She went outside to fetch the logs, following the path further round. Beyond a tall old hazel shrub, once coppiced, the outlines of a long straight garden lay in the pale moonlight. It was too late to explore any further than the log store now, but she knew from the agent's description that a footpath ran past the end of the garden, across the fields and joined an abandoned coaching road, now a green lane, running along the foot of the Downs.

Glancing once more at the silhouettes of oaks and chestnuts, which she guessed marked the end of the garden, she returned inside, locking the door and noticing that it had its heavy old original iron bolts, which she drew across. But there was a modern mortice lock. "Ah, a concession to the twenty-first century," Alice smiled to herself as she locked the door and put the key on the kitchen shelf.

After supper, she found a book of local history on the small oak rack in the sitting room and settled down to read. The air seemed to have cooled rapidly and she put more logs on the fire. "I'll read here for a while before I go up to bed," she decided. As she curled up on the sofa, the candle on the table flickered and she imagined she fleetingly glimpsed a dark shape in the corner of the room.

Alice started. She switched on the electric lamp and looked all round. There was nothing to be seen or heard. She returned to her reading. Suddenly she heard a faint scuffling. It seemed close by. She listened again. Was that scratching? Field mice, perhaps, or a badger outside. She strained to hear but the sound was not repeated. Soon she was absorbed by the book. As she had hoped, it did include references to the nearby village and even mentioned the hamlet though none of the houses were named individually. The area had been notorious as a bolt-hole for smugglers in the eighteenth century and it was believed that the remains of the entrance to a smugglers' tunnel lay beneath one of the cottages.

It was past midnight when she put down the book and went upstairs. The polished floorboards reflected the soft lamplight. The limewashed walls and massive oak beams gave her a feeling of contentment and belonging. She pulled up the heavy brocade bedspread and was soon asleep.

Much later – she was not sure when – she woke from a deep sleep. She had been disturbed by a piercing shriek but now there was deep silence. She switched on the bedside lamp. "Did I hear a scream or imagine it?" she wondered. Now fully awake, she could not be sure. She glanced round the room. "It must have been a fox," she thought. "They can sound ghastly."

After a few minutes she turned off the light and fell asleep, but this time with a slight feeling of unease, of something she could not quite explain.

Sometime later she was woken again. Now she felt a deep sense of dread. She heard a low rumbling sound, almost like the wind echoing down the chimney, but there was no wind outside. There seemed to be a faint greyish light seeping round the chintz curtains. "Thank God, the dawn," she thought but the feeling of dread intensified. Trembling, she reached out to switch on the bedside lamp but it was dead. "A power cut..." Fear raced through her mind. A feeling of horror washed over her and in spite of the darkness she knew she must get up and leave that room.

She felt her way downstairs. Trying to stay calm but not daring to look back she closed the wooden door at the foot of the staircase. For a moment in the sitting room the horror she had felt upstairs lessened, then suddenly she sensed again the dark shape in the corner of the room. It did not move but some instinct seemed to warn her that by its presence she would be trapped inside the house. She knew that she must escape now, must get outside before it was too late.

The cold in the kitchen reminded her that she had only a thin dressing gown. Her heart was pounding as she found her outdoor coat, tugged it on and drew back the bolts on the door. Fumbling in the dark, she found the key on the shelf and pushed it into the lock, trying desperately to open the door. But the key did not fit.

Alice was almost overwhelmed by fear. Why did the key not fit? In the gloom, the lock looked much older than she had remembered. Now black shadows seemed to be encroaching as if to grasp her and the feeling of horror and panic at being trapped washed over her again. The low rumbling began again, then got louder. It seemed to be approaching as she tried to escape the compelling, malignant force.

Still Alice struggled with the lock. Time was running out. As the noise grew deafening she looked round. Then her head span and she fell unconscious by the door.

When she awoke all was quiet. She was upstairs in bed and now a golden glow round the window showed that the low winter sun was shining outside. She drew back the curtains and looked out. The view was stunning, the fields along the foot of the Downs bathed in the light, the clear delicate blue sky with a scattering of wispy white clouds and the deep green shadows in the folds of the hills. Suddenly she remembered – she had had a terrible dream. The memory was fragmented and she felt unease without knowing why. "Did I go downstairs?" she wondered. "What happened down there?" Now, she knew she must go down, awake. Hesitantly, she made her way down the stairs.

All was calm and the sun was streaming in through the kitchen window. The colours in the garden were brilliant in the light and a heavy dew sparkled on the lawn. A pair of starlings was pecking for grubs. The door was locked but the bolts were drawn back. The key she had used to lock the door the previous evening was on the shelf. She took it and opened the door.

Outside, the winter air was crisp and still. After a quick breakfast, she packed hastily and put her things back in the car. She rang her friend Deborah and asked if it would be convenient if she came that afternoon, and spent Saturday night with her. "Why yes of course," Deborah replied. "You can make yourself at home here. I might have some work to do this afternoon but there are plenty of books or you could watch a film."

Alice took a last look around, locked the cottage, drove back up the lane and returned the key.

"I am very sorry but I have had to change my plans slightly and won't be staying tonight after all." She thought the caretaker looked at her curiously.

"Was everything alright?" she asked.

"Yes," Alice replied. "Thank you." She decided not to ask anything further about the cottage.

By the evening, settled in Deborah's drawing room, with a glass of wine at her side, the horror and dread of the previous night seemed to be fading. It had all been imagination, a nightmare. "Alice," her friend's voice interrupted her thoughts; she looked up. "I'm sorry, I was miles away..."

"Yes, I could see, you did seem a little distracted. Don't worry, I was just asking where it was – the cottage you rented last night?"

Alice repeated the names of the hamlet and the cottage. Her friend frowned slightly. "Well, that's a coincidence. You remember I was on the care home Committee some years ago. Well, one of our residents was an old lady who used to own that cottage. She is dead now of course, it was quite some time ago. But I remember a few months before she died she did mention that cottage – something had occurred there that seemed to have upset her. She wouldn't say exactly what, and it made no sense to us. All she said was "I saw it all. I could not get away. I was trapped as he was."

Alice started and Deborah saw the colour drain from her face. She took a deep draught of the wine, and stared at Deborah, as if in shock. She realised that in turn Deborah was looking at her with a puzzled expression; thoughts raced through her head – had the experience last night been real? Should she describe it to her friend? What was the force she had felt in the cottage? Would talking about it somehow resurrect it or in some way lay it to rest? What did it all mean, and worst of all – was it still pursuing her?

As she sat, indecisive, Deborah spoke again. "I can see something is troubling you and I suppose it has to do with that cottage. Did something happen last night? Can't you tell me?" Alice remained quite still in an agony of indecision. Then the memory of the previous night overwhelmed her and she broke down in tears. "I'm sorry, I can't tell you, it was awful," she sobbed. "I had a terrible nightmare and it seems to have affected me badly... I just can't get it out of my mind. But I want to try to forget it and enjoy the rest of the weekend. I don't want it preying on my mind when I have to go back to work on Monday."

Deborah's curiosity was aroused but she could see that it would be best not to ask any more just then. Instead she changed the subject and gradually Alice relaxed. After a good dinner they sat talking and catching up on their news; the next day was sunny again and after a brisk walk they had lunch in a country pub. By the time she was leaving to return to London, Alice seemed her old self and the memories of the cottage were fading.

A few weeks later, she was surprised to receive an email from Deborah.

Dear Alice, just wanted to say how much I enjoyed your visit and it was great to catch up on all the news. I hope you don't mind me mentioning this but I thought you might be interested. I happened to run into John P___ – you remember it was his mother that owned that cottage at one time. I couldn't help asking him if his mother had ever explained anything about it to him. He said no, but there was one curious thing. After she died, he found a copy of a very old newspaper cutting among her papers. She was interested in local history and she must have come across this. It was dated 14 December 1821 and entitled "Tragedy at Tap Cottage". It reported briefly that a suspected smuggler locked into the cottage while trying to escape the Customs Officers had been followed into a tunnel by one of them. A scuffle broke out and somehow the roof and walls of the tunnel which was also partly flooded by heavy winter rain had collapsed, burying the smuggler. The Customs Officer had barely escaped with his life but had managed to struggle free and get out. The trapped smuggler had tried to hold him down to be buried with him and it was claimed the Officer never recovered from the shock. John said his mother had never mentioned this story, but he had realised that often around mid-December she had found excuses to visit friends or stay with him, away from her cottage.

Alice drew a deep breath and deleted the email.

A DAY FOR SCHEMES
Barbara Day

'Martin's big brother brought us home from school again Mummy!' Karen's small daughter bounded into the kitchen. 'What's for tea?

'Egg and chips, so you can sit at the table right away. I'm dishing up', replied her mother.

This, reflected Karen, must be the umpteenth time in a week that young Mandy had made reference to the older brother in the Hargrave family.

'Making a habit of it is he? Well that's one way of getting you home for a change'.

As a general rule both children made their own way home from junior school. Once past the lollipop lady it was only a matter of yards up Knowles View to the corner flat opposite Martin's house.

Karen tended to forget any existence of an older brother. Since moving onto the new housing estate just over a year ago she'd not made his acquaintance.

'What's his name – Dave – isn't he working now'? Karen placed the meal before her daughter, ravenous as usual on her return from school.

'Don't think so. He's been decorating. They let me see, Mummy, it's fabulous!' she enthused between mouthfuls. 'He fixed a Christmas scene to their wall. It's a 'Muriel', he says it lights up. Wish we could have one'.

'What, you mean it's a 'mural'?' replied Karen.' Mrs Hargrave is lucky having a capable pair of hands around.'

Karen stifled any pangs of envy, aware that her own ambitious schemes had to go on hold for the time being. Going it alone meant doing without the little luxuries for a while. They'd been excited, getting the keys to the brand new flat. Even though, it had meant getting the furniture on HP. Karen was proud of her flair for furnishing. Of one thing she was certain, this Christmas was going to be special. No more Christmases spent with the in-laws, thank goodness!

The click from the auto switch on the kettle interrupted her reverie. Pouring out tea she summed up tasks on hand for the weekend now upon them. Christmas too was just around the corner.

'Whilst I think of it,' began Karen, once the meal was cleared away, 'I've got the painting to finish, then the new wallpaper to put up in the lounge this weekend, in case you'd forgotten. I shall want you out of my way you know!'

'I've promised to spend tomorrow with the Hargraves, Mummy, so I shan't be in your way.'

True to her word, Mandy took herself off next morning directly after breakfast was over.

'See you later,' she shrilled from the hallway endeavouring to extricate her cycle through the front door.

'Now mind you're home for lunch when the Hargraves have theirs,' warned Karen, grimacing at the impact twixt handlebars and the door handle. She sighed, would she ever learn to open the door wide enough? Mandy had little time for such trivialities, reinforced with sweets and matters more urgent to a seven year old.

Saturday came and went. Karen's paint brush flew and the lounge responded with a fresh gleam. Sunday she assigned to the papering. With luck, she'd be finished by lunch time. Not too daunting, she'd enjoyed helping Mike decorate his parent's house once.

The children called for Mandy and Karen was left in peace. Straight new walls meant simple work decided Karen and progressed well.

Later she congratulated herself on a job well done over a well- earned coffee. Next, a speedy clear up, followed by a quick silky shirt. Finally, what to make for tea? Something on toast would be easy. Ha, the breadbin was empty! That young rascal of hers had taken the last slice. Kept quiet, no doubt, to escape a mission to fetch more. Little monkey, she'd get a piece of her mind when she got home. She'd have to fetch some herself, perish the thought. One good thing, there was always a corner shop open on a Sunday in the older streets at the back.

Where the common linked the older area with the new, a cinder path led beside the recreation ground where the children played from both the old and new streets. Dusk was falling on her return, and from a gap in the hedge along the path, voices filled the air with childlike chatter. A group of kids spilled out onto the path before her.

'Mummy!' her daughter appeared accompanied by the Hargrave youngsters. Karen made out a tall stranger bringing up the rear, one arm held aloft, a small child on his shoulder – this Karen recognised to be little Alice Hargrave. At his heels trotted two chow dogs, known to be the apple of his eye. Karen wondered...

'Mummy look – THIS is David, Martin's big brother!'

The stranger's face immediately relaxed into a disarming smile. Jet black hair and striking brown eyes bore unmistakable resemblance to the Hargrave clan. Steadying the child on his shoulder, his free arm extended towards Karen in greeting. A suntanned hand reached out to her.

'Hi, so you're Mandy's mum then? We hear lots about you.'

Karen blushed slightly and returned the 'Hi' almost voicing her thoughts that she jolly well hoped all they heard was good.

The kids engulfed her, all chattering at once. A football kicked along by Martin crossed her path now and again, to be aimed back by one or the other of them. Next, the dogs were getting under her feet, or was it she who was under theirs? So this, reflected Karen, is Martin's older brother.

'David's been playing ball with us Mummy. We've had great fun,' was her child's retort.

David stepped back to join her. 'I've been hearing about this decorating of yours,' he grinned. 'Taken quite a job on yourself there, haven't you!'

'You mean my attempts at decorating,' laughed Karen. Her account of it seemed to amuse him. 'Hard slog, but well worthwhile when you see the results,' he agreed.

Reaching the boundary road of the estate, he transferred little Alice to an older sister and summoned them to wait until nodding his approval for them to cross safely.

Making a wild bid for home, they dashed ahead. Where their paths divided, Karen was about to bid him farewell when she noticed he hesitated. 'You know,' he began I'd rather like to see this handiwork of yours!' Karen was pleasantly surprised.

'Why not come and see for yourself?' That's as long as you promise not to pull me up on any mistakes,' she warned smiling. He winked at Mandy with a chuckle.

'We shan't criticise anything. We'll just tell you where you've gone wrong, won't we Mandy?' Karen warmed to his mischievous sense of fun.

Once inside the flat David approved of her efforts.

'Must say, you've got a good eye for colour schemes!' was his comment later over the coffee he accepted. 'That's a nice cocktail bar you have there,' he remarked. She had switched on its concealed lighting to enhance the wallpaper and this was now absorbing his attention. It created the soft, relaxing atmosphere she felt epitomised the very meaning of 'home'.

Stroking his chin thoughtfully he surveyed the wall behind it, as he paced to and fro. 'You'd never guess, but there's something missing here!' he declared glancing at Mandy, with a knowing wink. 'What's missing on this wall is a mural, don't you agree Mandy, something like ours?'

Mandy turned eagerly to Karen. 'Mummy, please!' she implored.

'I wouldn't take anything in the way of payment of course. I like to be occupied, doing something useful when I'm not working. Besides, it would be worth it just to see young Mandy's face. She's never stopped chattering about ours you know.' Karen knew all too well.

'Well-er-it sounds a lovely idea,' she faltered.

'You approve then? That settles it,' he announced triumphantly. 'I can start straight away if you like, in good time for Christmas. There's wood enough left from ours for a pelmet we need to take concealed lights. The lighting we can borrow from the bar for now and replace that later.'

Karen readily agreed. Though she was not to know it, the young man had heard a fair amount about Mandy's mum from the children. Hadn't he long been curious to meet her, having liked all he had heard? They agreed that, for her part, Karen would select a Christmassy scene for the mural, in town the next day. Dave promised he would make a start on Tuesday.

He glanced at his watch. 'Must dash now. Tea will be ready, Mum moaning about where I've got to!' The dogs at his feet shot forward to accompany him. 'Shall I look in tomorrow and pick up that spare key as arranged?' he called over his shoulder.

'There goes a charming young man,' was Karen's comment.

'Told you Mummy!' beamed her daughter.

The mural depicting a reindeer in full sprint over snow with a laughing Santa at the helm send Mandy wild with delight.

Karen jogged her memory for past reference made to Dave Hargrave, by his family. Doubtless any previous mention would have passed unnoticed at the time but now she was curious. Recollection dawned. Hadn't the children been over the previous Christmas, excitedly describing their presents to her? They'd told of a dolls house and cot, fashioned by David, their big brother, for the little ones. That apparently to ease the financial burden on parents, whose task at Christmas was no meagre one. A really good sort concluded Karen, one ready to help those less able to help themselves. She had no qualms about leaving the young man her key.

At last, with the mural in place, complete with illumination at the press of a switch. David collected the children from school ready to display the handiwork they had been impatient to see.

'I just love it,' young Mandy repeated over and over.

Karen, taking time out for Christmas shopping, with Dave in charge at the flat, was to be surprised on her return. 'It's perfect!' came her response. David was immensely satisfied, for Karen's face said it all.

The evening before Christmas found Karen putting up the final touches to the Christmas tree. Mandy had taken herself off to a party. The cards were in place and the fire burning to a glow. The mural was working its magic, now radiating Christmas cheer around, reflecting upon the baubles and glitter on the tree.

The shrill of the doorbell broke the silence. Who, Karen asked herself, would call at teatime, snow falling thick and fast, dusk descending? She noticed the shadow behind the glass of the front door was tall. On opening it, she discovered the figure of a young man clad in a black trench coat, collar turned up, particles of snow glistening on dark hair. Leaning against the door frame, stooping slightly to meet her gaze, stood Dave.

'Hi,' his expression dissolved into the friendliest of smiles. 'Just dropped by on my way home to leave you these. Thought they'd come in useful for that bar of yours!'

Karen was pleasantly taken aback. 'What a surprise, come in', she led the way in. Nodding towards the cocktail bar. 'Thanks, help yourself to a drink, there's lager and you can pour me a sherry if you will.'

The package she revealed to contain wine mats of different colours. 'I happened to be ain a craft shop and spotted them,' he explained.

'They're super, just what we needed for Christmas drinks,' she agreed.

Karen had sat down on the settee to inspect the mats when he joined her there, handing over her sherry as he did so. The heat from the fire offered sweet respite from the freezing weather outside.

The dark eyes were dancing with merriment when he turned, leaning in her direction to clink glasses in a toast. 'Here's to a Merry Christmas!' he announced, adding mischievously, 'May murals everywhere enjoy a successful New Year.' A shudder ran through Karen, feeling the warmth from the fire and a piquant sensation of sherry, a delightful combination. 'As it's Christmas,' he smiled, 'would you mind if I kissed you?'

From her position where he had leaned forward to clink her glass, Karen found herself gazing into the depths of those intense brown eyes, so close as to present an unfair challenge. With eyes closed, she sensed blissful awareness of his lips, ice cold and still damp from the snow, or was it perhaps the lager?

As the kiss lingered, it seemed to last for an eternity, every bit as intoxicating as the glass of sherry now tilted in her grasp, and quite as enchanting as the mural that had brought them together. Call it what she may, Karen could not recall any sensation where she felt more blissfully content.

The nicest thing of all about murals, Karen told herself, what the way they had of bringing people together. She was glad he thought of the scheme. Then, she concluded, how the plans that involved the happiness of others were all the more fulfilling.

Somehow, she decided, they were the schemes that always brought about happy endings.

TO SING OF MIDWINTER
Lorraine Hayward

It is freezing. The moon an icy ball suspended in a blue-black sky. Casts its biting light through a lace of glistening branches, a tracery upon the white ground, where small quick steps trace also. Claws and pads. He pads, his hunger as sharp as the air, the air as sharp as his bite. But will he use it this night? He uses his nose. He ducks through raw bramble, leaves behind a token of burnished red, betrays his passing. We see him emerge, trot across a silvered field. We anticipate his path to a window where a small light burns. Does the promise of warmth draw him as it might draw us? Do we wonder who does not sleep, so late, on a night so cold?

We might wonder. It is what we once called Twelfth Night. A last celebration of the nativity: feast and festivity, a last thumbing to the winter before the thrust of January's privations. But now we and our fox both will seek such solace in vain. Christmas was banned by Parliament, in sub-committee on a summer's day in 1647. Revolutionary bureaucracy the conclusion of reformatory zeal. Perhaps in June men forget how the cheer of Christmas weakens winter's grip. Sustains the poor, eases the conscience of the rich. Warms cockles for a short time before the resumption of cold and daily struggle.

We take a glimpse through the window. We do not intend to spy. A dog lifts his ears, gives a small, half-hearted start. *Who goes there?* The doorway a sudden slice of soft light. The dog runs out. Stops sharp. He has it. A pungent odour carried on pristine air. Twirls twice and finds. He sniffs at fox's footsteps. Lifts a leg, here, there. While he is preoccupied we can peek inside. There is a good fire and the aroma of roast. A call. *Jack, in, Jack.* The dog is obedient to the lure of the hearth. So we slip over the threshold in a canine wake and the door closes out the chill.

A candle burns on a small table. By the candle the Bible is closed, just. She is dressed like a godly woman. He like a godly man. A moment ago, God was with them in this room, in quiet Word. Now she bustles, setting out bread and plates. He closes his eyes, stretches his legs into the hearth. The dog shifts, makes room. They both begin a quiet snore. Dog's a breathy grumble. His a small grunt.

She, we will call her Beth, picks from a basket a contraband of holly leaves, red berries swollen. She ties them up while her husband sleeps. Above the fire, over the door. We read Beth's thoughts. Let him roar when he wakes. He fears punishment. By the law or the Lord? She is not sure which. Earthly censure is closer by. It is not her concern. Such we are taught, that all men are predestined for heaven or hell, her destination fulfilled all too soon. She has nothing left to fear.

She hears, and reads in the pamphlets which flutter around peoples' lives, of a world turned upside down. Where the church has become a battle ground. Where a king is imprisoned and charged with treason. Of fathers, sons, brothers in conflict; a fratricidal philosophy that tears a kingdom nearly in half. Over what? A king's prerogative to raise taxes to fund war? And in retaliation a vengeful Parliament wages war. And her sons die in a fury of discord over fiscal policy. When powerful men disagree, they hoodwink, bamboozle, bring God into it. She sees but cannot see her boys' bodies maimed, mud spattered, blood spattered. And in the name of who's God? The God of Rome or the Reformed Church? She has no preference.

The holly leaves prick her skin, as sorrow pricks at her heart. A heart gorged with grief, as swollen as the berries. Berries as Christ's blood? A popish image she must throw away. It is no hardship. She sees only the blood of her sons in a symbol of nature's promise. There is no comfort to be found in the dry pages of King James's book. She seeks now a more visceral creed. For what in truth do we believe? What we are told to believe at some point or other? This winter celebration has ever been nothing more than a pagan ritual. What is it to do with God or not to do with him? And if man declares she cannot celebrate the birth of Christ then let her sing of midwinter and rebirth. Let her be hung for a sheep as a lamb.

Beth glances at her sleeping husband. Whispers a command. The dog rises, follows. And we, compelled to discover her scheme, must stalk after him once more through the door.

She steps out into winter's vicious welcome. He greets her with a bite on tear-worn cheeks and snaps at hands wrung dry with grief. Within her cloak a knife's blade colds. She is grateful for the moon's light, so bright she casts a shadow before her. About her feet, the dog heels then bounds. Rejoices in the familiar route. A path to the place where her boys once played, tamed a hawk, teased a puppy. A stand of trees. She passes under the low arms of the guardian of the copse. The oak who hugs a mantle of brittle rust, leaves which keep a tentative grasp until spring's embrace warms his bark. In a small breath of wind they declaim his mighty presence. Then silence returns. She circles her way through the family of birch trees, slender, fine sons and daughters, who revel in the moon, their very being a reflection of his light. At the foot of a tall and ancient elm swathed in a pall of ivy she stops, turns around. Raises her eyes into the filigree of branches. Stars peep through, bright as pins. This is the place she will keep her vigil.

She lights a stub of candle she has brought. In a small bowl she burns a fire of twigs. She hesitates a while. Recalls the words taught to her quietly as a girl by the women of her village, those who healed, who brought forth children, skilled in herbs and secrets of the Earth. A song of spring and winter, of decline and resurrection, of life over death. She watches the small flames rise then die. Begins to sing clear imperfect notes into the night.

Darkness falls
The land is hard
No leaf, no flower
Life's heart in shards
You are gone
But as summer's breeze
You will blow
Come back to me

Her voice falters as the candle flame flickers. A velvet presence brushes her scalp, a gentle stroke of her hair. A shape slides through the freezing air, motion silent as the night. She perceives rather than sees his passing. Wings soft as cotton, breast snowy as down. He alights on a low branch. Her breast is beating, rising. She twists, turns, surveys. *Where are my boys?* Looks back to wise eyes which catch in the moonshine. Eyes which blink only a question in return before he soundlessly lifts. She follows his flight through limbs and branches out into the frozen fields. As he hunts, so must she. Takes up her song.

Rise King of Oak
O'er King of Holly
Heed mankind's fate
Heed mankind's folly
Awake the earth
From winter's sleep
So cold below the ground
Come back to me

A rustle in the quiet. Her eye is drawn to the ground where a spiny form struggles out from under frosted leaves. A tiny nose tests the air. Little feet stretch as if from sleep. She has awoken him, this small, spiked creature, disturbed his winter rest. Her power is growing. Heartened, she adds to the fire. Watches the hog wander in disdain from the warm light into the shadows and raises her voice again.

Gone longest night
Day born anew
Awake the god
Of the rising sun
Warm frozen earth
And fill her womb
Dark to light, life returns
Come back to me

What is it that makes Beth start and turn in the silence after her song? It is no external sense. There are other senses. Ones which man has forgotten to use. The dog in his animal wisdom lifts his head. Sniffs, searches the air. A scent he knows. Stands, stares. Ears pricked, eyes keener than hers in the dark. Beth tracks his gaze. *Boys? My boys?* And through the crisped fern and thorny bramble a swift shape comes forth. Halts sharp before them. Surprised, it seems, that he is come upon these two others. Others he should shun and avoid. The fox regards them. Regards her. Fixes her with his presence. And in that moment she knows his warmth, his vigour. Comprehends his corporeal beauty. Shares his vitality, feels the essence of his mortality. For he is of the Earth, as she is of the Earth. As her sons are of the Earth. That both life and death are a single test that all nature's creatures must endure. And she fears for him, this handsome, vulnerable beast. For his survival in these harshest of times. Stretches out an arm of comfort. *Come. Here.*

The spell is broken. The dog starts. *Stay, Jack!* An order. The fox turns, darts through the copse. Gone. She sighs, saddened, bereft. She has no song left. Her candle will soon fail. She has nothing but fingers which curl around a blade.

But then a brief glimpse. She sees him again. A sleek silhouette trots along the moonlit path. He stops, short. Cocks his head as if to hear. Glances to the brow of the lane. Quickens in alarm. A glance back. His eye catches hers as he ducks under the hedge. Vanishes.

She turns her gaze to see what his sharp ears have caught. Strains her eyes to the shadowy distance, breath held. Two figures, one smaller than the other, dim, mist-wreathed, approach quietly out of the dark. Her heart stops then pounds. One strides out, the other lags slightly, trots to catch up. Lags, trots. Lags, trots. She feels her spirit fill with a blessed memory. Joy courses through her body. A gentle breeze rises. On its lee there is a sound, familiar but strange. The hum of bees, the buzz of the hoverfly. And there are her sons as small boys, the older leading, the younger dangling at his brother's hind. Yellow hair bouncing in the sun. *Wait, Joseph, wait for me.* A run, a chase. Laughter in green, warm light, through swinging grasses, under dappled boughs and a lark's sweet reel. In their wake, Beth strolls, smiling at their game, summer soft on her skin. Calls them to her. *Joseph, Thomas!* Leads them homeward in balmy contentment. Strolls out under the trees into the lane.

The nearing figures halt, hesitate. The smaller steps forward, more quickly but with an awkward, difficult gait. "Mother?" A gentle voice brushes aside sunshine and ease. "Mother?" Winter night grasps once more. Moon. Ice. Bitter cold. And Beth's tears roll as her daughter, large with child, takes her hands. "We have come to keep Twelfth Night with you. Why are you out here so late?"

"Oh, my girl." Beth turns away. Hides both her grief and her love. "I have come to gather some ivy." She takes out the knife from under her cloak. At the foot of the mighty elm, cuts the cold, dark leaves. Evergreen. Ever-lasting. She does not know if she takes joy or pity in the prospect. But she takes now what she can get. Takes leave of the place that held her hope. Takes her daughter's arm.

The three step towards the warm light of the house. Beth keeps her counsel. The dog makes merry with his new companions. And a sharp nose, obscured, secreted, witnesses their passing.

We watch them enter. This time we will not intrude. Through the window we see her husband stir from his chair. He embraces his daughter, takes the hand of his son-in-law. Remarks the strung holly, his wife's hands, full of ivy. Enfolds them briefly in his. They share small, heavy smiles. Put cares aside as the feast is set. And with a muted toast they settle to eat.

Perhaps we should make report of what we have seen this night. But we do not think we will. For there are many things in life which neither learning nor faith can describe. And it is hard to lose the spirit of Christmas. It is harder to lose your sons. We may lose a king. But winter will always return.

ANOTHER ROOM
George Matthews

It was winter, and the setting sun had set fire to the western sky, creating a sore crimson backcloth that transformed the elegant spire of the ancient church into a sinister black fingerpost that pointed to the heavens.

And so Captain Farnol rode his hireling at a gentle walk through the deserted village.

Darkness had finally supplanted the setting sun, and pools of light from the flanking cottages began to seep onto the road, and the tang of woodsmoke lingered on the cold air that was still and threatened frost.

The steel shod hoofs of the horse echoed with a soporific rhythm as they hacked along the deserted street, and the rhythm induced a mood that was both melancholic and meditative, and the captain was much given to meditation of late. Who are we? Where do we come from? Where are we going? Where indeed? The padre had spoken piously of the other side, but was unable to explain just what the other side might be. On the other hand Field Marshal Haig had once written with gross insensitivity that...

'We lament too much over death. We should regard it as a welcome change to another room.'

Farnol could only marvel that the architect of the apocalyptic battles of the Somme and third Ypres could pontificate in such an ill-considered manner. Ensconced in his chateau miles behind the front lines, he appeared oblivious to the holocaust taking place in the trenches. But what of Haig's other room?' Would there even be another room? If so what would it be like? The enigma fascinated him. He was not afraid of death, simply curious of its aftermath. He had spent three years in the trenches, and his original company of seventy had been reduced to three. They were being replaced however by a steady influx of conscripts, callow boys from the farms and industrial cities, cannon fodder for Haig's meat grinder.

In an effort to dispel these melancholy thoughts he recalled the latest Joe Miller circulating the trenches.

It appeared that Haig venturing forth on one of his rare visits to the forward areas was anxious to visit the newly arrived Australian contingent, having been advised by sycophantic staffers that although their courage and fighting abilities were beyond question, their 'dedication' might not be.

'Have you come here to die?' Haig enquired fatuously of a small scruffy figure. The Aussie peeled himself off the wall, flicked away his roll-up and replied.

'No mate. We came 'ere yeserdie.'

Smiling, Farnol rode under the arch that led into the yard of the coaching inn. The yard was illuminated by many lamps, and several intelligent equine heads with ears ricked, studied him as he stiffly dismounted. A groom appeared immediately, enquired if the captain had had a good day, and led the horse into one of the boxes that surrounded the yard. Farnol followed them into the box which was clean and well littered. By the lantern's light he watched the old horse contentedly drink the gruel into which, following the captain's instructions, had been mixed with a bottle of stout. Only when the groom was engaged in the process of whisping the horse down did Farnol tip the groom and turn his attention to his own needs.

Before going up to his room he drank several glasses of toddy with the locals whilst discussing the day's sport. His room was at the end of a long dimly lit passage. There were two rooms at the end of the passage, one on each side. The rooms were numbered six and nine.

The sudden warmth of the bar and the several toddies had left the good captain somewhat befuddled, and as he stood holding his room key he was aware that attached to it was a large wooden label. The label bore the number six. Or was it a nine with a tail? He preferred the nine. His regiment was after all, the 9th Foot. Naturally it was the wrong door.

Nevertheless he was surprised to be greeted by a small, sharp featured man of medium height, attired in the dress of a bygone era. His well- cut hunting coat was full skirted, and adorned with huge silver buttons which were beautifully engraved with a running fox and the initials E.F.H. The man's breeches were snowy white, as was his neatly tied stock. His hair was greying at the temples, and tied at the nape of his neck. A neat workman-like figure. He extended his hand.

'Good evening sir, my name is Franklin. We have been expecting you.'

The situation had become so preternatural that Farnol, aware that he had little control over the circumstances, permitted events to run their course.

He was guided by the elbow to where several gentlemen were warming their backsides before a huge log fire. They were all attired in the long green coats with the huge silver buttons. The gentlemen were introduced, but within minutes, Farnol, in his slightly befuddled state could remember only that of his host.

'It is our custom,' Franklin announced. 'To gather at the end of the season we dine, sing and drink a little.'

Having eaten nothing since breakfast the dining part sounded particularly attractive to Farnol. A vast and varied supper was consumed, and a jolly atmosphere prevailed. Toasts were proposed, and a decanter of vast proportions made its not unhurried rounds.

Farnol balanced his chair on its back two legs, and puffed happily on a Burmese cheroot. He felt completely at ease in the company of these bluff countrymen, but he'd had a long day, and was beginning to feel the pace. This did not go unnoticed by his new companions, and to the accompaniment of loud cheers and much laughter, Farnol was carried to his room and dumped unceremoniously on his bed. They left as noisily as they had entered.

Franklin was the last to leave, and pausing in the doorway, he turned and said enigmatically. 'Goodnight my friend. We have enjoyed your company and will meet again when the time is right. Then we will welcome you not as a guest but a member.'

He closed the door softly behind him.

The following morning Farnol awoke with a head like a concertina, and a tongue like a button stick. Lying in the great bed he endeavoured to recall the events of the previous night. Had it been a dream? A fantasy? Or had he intruded upon some elaborate charade staged by wealthy, but eccentric sportsmen?

There was but one way to find out.

Pulling on his robe he left his room, and crossing the narrow passage knocked smartly on the door opposite. A door that bore the figure nine. Receiving no reply he turned the doorknob and eased open the door. As the door swung inwards he found himself in a small windowless cupboard smelling of soap and coal tar. Mops, brooms and buckets lined the walls. Gone the great fireplace and the noble festive board. Not a shred of evidence remained of the previous night's jollity. No sign of his new companions. He stepped back into the passage prior to closing the door. As he did so he observed something lying in the shadows. It was round, and had a familiar look which at first he could not identify. Thoughtfully he closed the cupboard door.

And so Captain Farnol's leave drew to a close. Dressed now in uniform he crossed the yard of the inn. It was a fine morning. There had been a heavy overnight frost, and the frost covered cobbles of the yard sparkled in the winter sunshine. Nearby, churchbells were summoning the faithful, and God was in his heaven.

Jasper, the captain's mount of the previous day, was standing with his wise old head over the barn door. Farnol walked across to the barn and patted the gelding's neck before feeding him some sugar filched from the breakfast table.

A trap was waiting to take Farnol to the station, and giving the horse a final pat on the neck he crossed the yard. In one hand he carried his valise. The other was deep in the pocket of his British warm, and the fingers of that hand were clasped tightly around a large silver button.

'…. We will meet again when the time is right.'

Captain Farnol was smiling. No longer would he ponder the mystery of life after death. He had discovered 'Another Room.'

THE WINTER OF DISCONTENT
Margaret A. Stevens

The whale had been enjoying itself with all its friends and family, but something had attracted it away from the rest and he had swum into shallow waters.

A sudden large wave had taken him right onto the sandy beach, well above the water line. He lay waiting for the sea to lash over him to enable him to return to the water but nothing was happening. He lay there and suddenly realised that he was hoping in vain as he lay well up on the beach and there was no chance of returning to swim in the deep sea, diving and playing with the other young whales, as by now the tide was going out and the beach was growing larger and all he could see was large stretches of sand.

Before him was something very strange. It looked as if it could be a carol reef but it was straight and there were no fish swimming around it, only some small creatures moving around on the top of it.

These were actually people, part of a large crowd who were gathering to survey his predicament. Suddenly there was a loud wailing sound rather like the wind blowing above the waves when gales blew across the oceans he travelled in.

Creatures were now running around near to where he lay, but he couldn't escape because he was completely unable to move and anyway they were all so small that he didn't feel afraid of them, they were so insignificant as far as he was concerned. He thought there was a small sea worm being unrolled before and out of its mouth water was being splashed all over him.

He wasn't to know that this was the fire brigade which had been called to see if they could handle the situation and try to get him back into the sea.

He was glad of the cooling water that was being sprayed all over him from these coils of snakes and as this continued throughout the night, he began to feel a little refreshed. There were continual wailing sounds filling the air and signs of great activity going on all round him, everyone was trying their best to help this defenceless creature.

He really felt so helpless and hopeless and had no way of getting himself out of his predicament and there seemed to be no way for him to get him down the beach and back into the sea.

He felt that all was lost and that he would just have to stay there for the rest of his life. The little creatures buzzing round him seemed to not be of any use and although they had tied ropes around him and tried to pull him over the sands to the water's edge, their efforts had all been in vain.

Darkness was all around him and the air was cooler but the hoped for wave just wasn't coming. The tide was still out and there didn't seem any chance of a wave large enough to come to his rescue.

The activity around him stopped, although he was still being sprayed by these worm-like beings and they seemed to have an abundance of water coming out of them. Some large strange objects were digging out a trench to the sea.

Charlie looked at the letter he had just received from his Managing Director.

It really didn't say very much. Just to tell him that the owner of the firm was visiting the factory where he worked and wanted to have a word with Charlie when he came.

Charlie was now in his late 50s and he knew that there were younger men than him joining the firm, some of whom had been to University and were certainly more learned about modern methods than he was.

That night he couldn't sleep. Eleanor, Charlie's wife was aware of him tossing all night and heard him finally get up and go downstairs when the clock was only saying 4.30 a.m.

In the morning Charlie decided to go for a walk along the seafront, near to where he lived. He saw the crowds gathered along the se wall and several fire brigades gathered and on the beach lay a large whale, nearly covered in sand and a large digger trying to dig out a pathway down to the sea. A team of firemen were directing their hoses onto the whale so that a constant stream of water was surrounding it.

He looked at the face of the whale and its doleful expression mirrored his own. It certainly didn't look as if it was enjoying itself and obviously was in a situation that was most unpleasant.

"Just like him," he thought. He certainly didn't like the fact that in a few days' time he was to stand before the owner of the firm he worked for and goodness only knew what was going to be said to him.

"Sorry! Charlie. We know you have been with us since you were a boy, but times move on and modern methods are being brought in, for which you have no training, and we are anxious to move into the 20th century. Of course we shall offer you a pension, although this might not be very large, as you may still be able to find employment elsewhere which will be more suited to your abilities."

He could see himself standing, cap in hand thanking Mr. Blowers for his generosity and walking out of the office to be unemployed and with little money to continue paying his mortgage, taking holidays abroad and running the new car he had just bought.

When he returned home his wife had cooked him his usual Sunday morning breakfast of sausages, bacon, eggs, tomatoes, mushrooms and toast, and as he sat down, Stella, his youngest daughter who was still living at home placed a hot steaming cup of coffee next to him. She wrapped her arms round him and kissing the top of his head she told him what a lovely Dad she thought he was and thanked him for paying her college fees.

He found he was being pampered all day and showered with favours such as he hadn't known for a long while. Later Brenda, his eldest daughter arrived with her two children Robin and Faye and they were on their best behaviour, even asking if he would like them to do some jobs in the garden.

He thought about the whale lying there, feeling sorry for itself, and of all the ministrations that were being handed out to him by the firemen and others who were doing their best to keep it alive and trying to make him as comfortable as possible.

He had a sudden surge of gratitude to his family for their good intentions as they realised how worried he was about the forthcoming interview and he wondered if the whale was appreciating all his comforter's efforts on his behalf.

The day of the interview dawned at last and he dressed with even greater care than was usual, putting on the spotted tie Eleanor had bought him for Christmas.

He strode down the path and opened the door of his new car, wondering how long he would be able to keep up the payments on it.

Pulling into the car park of the place where he worked, several men shouted to him.

"Good morning, Charlie!" Ben shouted.

"Had a good weekend, Charlie?" his Manager enquired.

This was instead of the usual grunt and half wave they gave him.

"Hullo. Charlie. You're looking particularly smart this morning," Betty from Accounts told him.

Did they all know that this could be the last time he would be arriving at work?

Had some of them been promised his job and they were just trying to be kind and sympathetic towards him, he thought.

He couldn't help but wonder about the whale he had seen previously and wondered if it had managed to slip back into the water and join the other fish in the sea. Did he thank those who had tried to make his miserable stay a little more acceptable? With this thought he waved back to the two men and remembered the good times they had shared together.

Mr. Phelps, the Senior Manager was waiting for him as he entered the building and immediately directed Charlie towards his office.

Seated at the desk, which seemed to fill all the room, was Mr. Thompson Jnr., the present owner. He stood to his feet as Charlie entered, reaching out a hand and saying,

"Congratulations Charlie. You have just been promoted to Assistant Senior Manager and you will be receiving a substantial pay rise starting from next week, if that's alright with you. Mr. Phelps is finding the work load a bit too much and he will be very pleased to be having extra help, particularly as we have been getting some good orders in recently, with promises of more to come. You had better collect your things from the workshop and get your new office ready to use. Mr. Phelps will fill you as to what he wants you to do. Will that suit you?"

"Well...thank you, Sir," Charlie stuttered. "That will be fine." He could hardly believe what he was hearing and he hurried out of the room to ring his wife and let her know the good news.

The next morning the people who had gathered to witness the whale as the poor creature lay very still, eyes occasionally opening and shutting, were sure that it was about to breathe it's last breath.

Suddenly its eyes opened wide. It could hear the sound of waves crashing in the distance and the sound was getting nearer and nearer. A large wave sent water cascading over his back and then another and then he felt water underneath his body.

Gently and gradually he was being dragged back down the beach towards where the waves were crashing on the sand and then he was lifted up into the air by a particularly large wave and pulled right out into the depths and he could manage to twist round and swim right out to the far horizon.

Loud cheering filled the air and firemen began to roll up their hoses. Diggers were making their way back onto the road and people began to drift away.

Returning home, after a most exciting and rewarding day, one that in his wildest dreams he could not have envisaged, Charlie saw that the crowds had left the sea front and the whale was no longer lying in its helpless state on the beach. Looking out to sea he could picture it swimming happily with it's family and friends, back where he wanted to be and with that he hastened his steps home, where all his family would be there to welcome him saying how pleased they were with the news he had received that day. Quite possibly Eleanor would have cooked him a special dinner and after, when all the family had left, they could settle down to a contended evening together.

THE LAST FATHER CHRISTMAS
Iris Pearson

My dear Child,

The ice is thinning, the sky is completely dark. My bristled beard is studded with flecks of frost. Under this tented-roof of sky I am the only one left. The Last Remaining. The final of the illustrious bloodline born to follow this single path. A line who knew their duty, welcomed the fact there was no scope for deviation. I embraced my role as just a link in a far-reaching chain. Who knew I would be the end of it? Let Saint Nicholas forgive me.

You, my dear child, were my very last hope. This Christmas Eve, a single present rests on my sleigh, the final one, wrapped carefully in shiny silver paper. The sleigh is rusted now; flakes of paint drift on to the untrammelled snow around it. And I think the present, too, is broken as somewhere inside, something rattles. But what does this matter to me now? The sleigh will not be needed after tonight. You are my final child.

My lungs are old and my joints are stiff; I fear my eyes may have lost their twinkle. The stubborn and skittish reindeer are puffing and snorting after even the short ride to this ridge. To think they were once the graceful, leaping creatures who girdled the earth in a single night. But their fitness is not important anymore either. I have only one present to deliver tonight, and that is yours. Forgive me if I let you down this year. Yours was the only letter that reached me, a bittersweet surprise, bringing with it hope but also the certainty that the day I always knew would come had finally arrived. It seems I am no longer needed.

Stretching back for generations, my family have survived in the harshest environments, North of everywhere. Bar one day a year, we have been immune from the worst of this world. We have been blind witnesses to war, house fires, starving children. We were the cradle only for happy togetherness.

In this same log cabin my ancestors have toasted their bellies with bottles of brandy and warmed their feet by the fire. Kris Kringle, Papa Noel, Sinter Klaas, Grandfather Frost, Jultomten, Mikulas, Santa Claus, they have brought joy all over world since time began. And just as they had consumed their fill of mince pies and were ready to bid goodbye to the world, the next would be ready and willing to take over.

I remember my first Christmas in charge. The elves had to stack the sleigh and fasten the reindeer. With trepidation, I drew on the ancient berry-red coat for the first time and whisked the reindeer into the sky. The pattern of the stars that night are still etched in my memory, so anxious was I not to lose my way.

How things change. In those days, the workshops hummed with life, full of painting, packing, stitching and sticking, wrapping and sorting. The satisfaction of being part of something more important than presents made up for the bone-weariness.

But this year you are only one. No one nowadays wants a peculiar-shaped box with a train set inside. No little girl dreams of getting a doll from Father Christmas. Indulgences are commonplace; every day brings treats. The special treat that once was Christmas is tainted by a greedy shadow. Every year I deliver more but it seems never to be quite sufficient. As the presents have multiplied in number so their value seems to me to have been much diluted, dissolving by the steam of the turkey.

So this year, dear child, is the last. I am old, and there is no one to take over from me. Children do not need me anymore. Yours is my final present. I will dismiss the elves, release the reindeer, leave the sleigh to rust.

To you I reply, and to you I bid my final farewell. I cannot leave this place, nor can I stay. Humans are getting ever-closer, encroaching with their tourist boats and oil tankers.

I have my old boots and my coat, although it does not seems as warm as it once was, and the bottle with the last few mouthfuls of brandy, so that should keep me going for a while. And your letter, of course. I will go to the top of this great ridge and watch the Northern Lights streak the sky with purple and green. On Christmas Day this year, I will fish for whales.

Yours affectionately,
Christmas.

THE CHANGELINGS
Sheila Powell

It began with the card. The image had struck a chord somehow as if a memory had been evoked, something deep and distant, like a tiny pearl at the bottom of a muddy pool. She had looked at other cards several times and gone back to it. There was no price marked. The woman at the till had frowned, turned it over. Said it was odd, must be old stock, let her have it for a pound. There were no others. Once home, she had been reluctant to send it, wanted, irrationally, to keep it, but knew it was the perfect picture, that Jo, her intensely pagan friend, would love it too.

The image was of a white deer, stylised but strangely real, too, not brash with glitter but subtly dusted with something as fine as white pepper. The deer was elegant, fine-limbed, with the gentle look of a hind, yet it bore the antlers of a stag, antlers wreathed in mistletoe. The deer stood on an almost featureless hill, a smooth, shimmering dome. Behind it, a single tiny fir tree stood, a token concession, it seemed, to our modern day celebration of Christmas.

The card was blank and so she wrote,

"I am Oisin, Beloved of the Gods,
Beloved of the Earth,
Whose father was a Hunter,
Whose mother was a poet,
Who comes to you from an Unseen World
With a Message of Peace
And Love and Protection.

The words came easily and she felt a fluttering in her throat as she wrote them.

She sent the card a week before Christmas because, like her, Jo recognised December, from the twentieth onwards, as the month of the rebirth of the sun, a celebration of nature and new life.

When she went out to post it the world was in the grip of a cold so severe that every leaf and blade and twig was held fast, every surface sprouting hoar frost like a silver fungus, its crystals standing an inch high on the telephone wires. Indeed, it seemed the Ice Age 'had begun its heave.'

She stood uncertainly. At home there were jobs to be done, but they seemed irrelevant now. She thrust her hands into her pockets, frowning – then glanced wistfully back at the house she had grown to love. She crossed the road and quickly left it to follow an ancient track-way that led first between fields then between copses and marl pits, taking her deeper into the Narnian landscape. As she walked she listened to her own footfalls, could hear nothing else save the imagined beating of her heart. For as she walked the silence grew deeper, the world so still that it seemed no life existed but hers. She felt that the lane would go on forever and she would follow a path around the earth until she too became white and encrusted like the branches and stems, enmeshed in the icy web of the hoar frost. And the thought sent a tremor of excitement through her as if . . . as if . . she were going home. What was it about the silver trees that filled her with longing?

She stopped, lifted her head, stamped her feet, needing for a moment to feel the earth beneath them. A robin alighted on a frozen twig only feet away. He was the size of a tennis ball, his feathers fluffed out to keep the cold at bay. He cocked his head and whistled at her, then flew ahead to alight on another tree further up the lane.

She smiled and followed him until he flew up high into an alder tree. She watched him bobbing and flapping and whistling. Then he was gone, feather and bone and beautiful song, a tiny speck of warm, resilient life.

When she looked ahead again she saw the deer, just an impression at first, a trick of the light and the startling brightness of the snow conspiring to bend the shadows of empty winter boughs into something that was already in her head, filling her imagination. She saw what she wanted, half expected, to see. She closed her eyes and looked again. It was gone. She walked more quickly, carefully crossed a ditch to an embankment that rose between two murky ponds and stood, staring down at pale hoofprints in the smattering of snow. She bent to touch them with her fingertips. Then she looked up to where the lane disappeared around a bend – and there he was, no trick of the light this time.

Strains of Nimrod startled her, brought her back. She took out her mobile phone, saw Jo's name and put the phone to her ear, never taking her eyes from the white deer.

"Where are you?" her friend asked.

"Walking."

"Me too. Near the Tor. I'm looking at something I can't quite believe."

"I know. I see it too. I sent you a card …"

"Let me guess. A white deer on a hill. I bought one in Glastonbury yesterday. Now, our other selves will receive them."

"It's time, isn't it? That's what he's come to tell us. I didn't expect it so soon. So what do we do now?"

"Just keep walking, I guess. Have you said your goodbyes?"

She shook her head dumbly, then whispered, "How could I? I didn't know."

"Do you think they'll see the difference when the others return?"

"At first maybe, but it will soon pass. They have been programmed as we have."

"I wish we could return together, you and I."

"We are together, in spirit. Just think of what awaits us when we pass through the gateway. Do you remember the silver tree where birds forever sang – and the two moons and the meadows where we played...?"

"Of course... the silver tree... You're breaking up..."

She heard two more words ... "soon" ... and "gateway", and the connection was lost.

As she returned to the path, her foot slipped on the frozen mud. She flung out her arms and the mobile phone flew through the air and hit the ice of the pond. When she looked up the deer had gone. She returned to the path and continued walking. When she met her own image coming from the other direction she raised her eyes and attempted a smile. Her other self smiled in return and whispered, "It's beautiful, more beautiful than I had imagined, like a world built of crystal – but it all looks so fragile – as if a wind could shatter it."

She nodded and couldn't stop the tears. "I have done what I could. I have written and painted. I have planted and nurtured but there is so much to do here. They do not know what they have. They have forgotten to care for it."

For a brief moment their hands touched.

"How many of us are there?" she asked.

"Thousands."

"Enough to make a difference?"

The other smiled.

"Do you care that you were taken?"

"Oh no. Your world is what our world must strive to be."

"Good luck! May all the gods be with you."

They parted and she saw once again faint hoof prints in the snow – leading her onward to a shimmering hill beyond the common, a hill upon which was a single fir tree and a white deer whose antlers were wreathed in mistletoe.

WHILE HIS SOUL GENTLY WEEPS
Lynn Stewart

'Ho Jimmy, ye there, Jimmy?'

His name wasn't Jimmy, but he was there.

He listened to the voices travel down from the bridge and land underneath, where he sat.

'Oi, Jimmy Strummer, gie us a strum.'

He held the guitar in his hands but he didn't strum it.

'Give us a tune, on ye go.'

He didn't like to strum in front of people. Or pluck. He got embarrassed. The guitar was just for him. He held it in his hands but he didn't strum it.

Waiting until nobody could hear was tricky, because people walked over and past him every day. Some stared, most didn't. Some sneered, most didn't. Most looked away. Some threw loose change. He didn't play for money, but he would wait until the footsteps had evaporated before he picked it up all the same. Put it in his pocket for a rainy day.

His name wasn't Jimmy, Jimmy anything and definitely not Jimmy Strummer. He thought they probably meant Joe Strummer, but they weren't old enough to remember the 90s, never mind Joe Strummer. *He* was barely old enough to remember.

Broken memories of mouthy brothers, safety pins and a lot of blood came flooding into his mind. Tartan trousers, hair that should never have seen the light of day and faces you could hang things from. He was glad he was too young to do such things with safety pins. It wasn't natural for something with the word *safety* in it to produce so much blood. He was glad he only had to watch from the sidelines, from shadows filled with cigarette smoke and screams.

Maybe the boys did know about Joe Strummer, but Jimmy Strummer was what they shouted. They've never asked him his name. If they did ask, he wouldn't tell. He isn't sure he'd remember even if he wanted to. The life where he had a name was gone.

He found the guitar abandoned in the grass behind a wall a little way along the riverbank from his spot under the bridge. He picked up a guitar for the first time when he when he was in high school and had learned the G, D and E minor chords before giving up a week later. He wasn't good enough.

He thought maybe he could start learning again with this one. It only had four strings, but maybe that wouldn't matter too much. The one nearest the bottom and the second one from the top were missing. He didn't know what these strings were called, but he didn't suppose he needed to if they were missing. If they ain't there, they don't need names, because if they ain't there, they don't exist. Not anymore.

Not a breath of wind disturbed the glassy surface of the river but he noticed the frost nuzzling the grass and realised it was getting colder, telling him time was moving on. His fingers skimmed the frayed edges of the thin sleeping bag beneath him. Winter was coming. It might have come already for all he knew.

Days have melted into one. He used to count the sunrises, until he realised he didn't know what he was counting them for. He had nothing to look to or to aim for. So he stopped.

He didn't know how many days, weeks, months, or even centuries, of suns setting and rising had drifted past unnoticed since he left. Time didn't mean very much to him now.

He recalled a line from somewhere inside his memory, from a book he had read many times: *And how slow and still the time did drag along.*

He recalls getting lost in the pages as a child, sometimes wishing he could run away like Huck. Many years later he studied the same pages of the book he would get lost in as a child with the children who looked up at him as he stood at the front of the classroom, still wishing he could run away.

Be careful what you wish for.

Junkie. Alky. Manky. Tramp.

Just some of the words that were, at times, spat down upon him with venom from above. From the safety of the bridge. Not the same boys who called him Jimmy.

Different ones.

'Look at that alky, living under the pishy bridge. Is it cos of him it's called the pishy bridge? Bet it is.'

'Aye, bet it is.'

'Junkie.'

He couldn't stop his ears from hearing, though he tried to stop his brain from caring. He hung his head all the same.

Most times he melted into the background as life swerved to avoid him. In these times he could have believed he was invisible. But then the voices came. They reminded him he was not quite gone. He may have been standing with his back to life, on the very edge of existence, but he was still here. Just.

Strumming the guitar made his life more tangible; he was making sounds that existed, sounds that echoed. Under the bridge he was making sounds that could escape and dance with other sounds in the air.

He was not strumming for other people, but as a way of reminding himself, and the universe, that he was still in the world. Just. He liked the noise, and it kept him busy.

And if he pressed down hard enough, he could make his fingers bleed.

He used to bury the guitar in the grass and reeds behind him when the sky revealed it was night's turn to watch over him. Not now. He missed the feel of it, knowing it was the only thing that attached him to the world he felt even more lost when darkness came over him and this link was missing.

Sometimes he took his guitar and dragged his thin sleeping bag so he could lie with his head sticking out from underneath the bridge, where his eyes could get lost in black nothing peppered with stars, but he had to be careful he didn't let his mind wander and bump into any memories he was trying to elude. His brain had to stay numb, and strong. He couldn't allow the stars and their false hope to burrow in too deep. These stars were already dead, or dying.

He had to pull his sleeping bag tight when the moon whispered to him it was time to close his eyes. If sleep came, she never stayed long.

The frost on the grass seemed to be growing in front of his eyes and he could feel a nip from the morning air on his skin, but it didn't matter because the nice lady who always smiled should be coming soon. The nice lady who always smiled was something else that made him realise he was still, not alive exactly, but in this world at least. She sometimes walked past him in the evening too. He was always there to see her, because he didn't have anywhere else to be.

He never smiled back. He couldn't. He didn't deserve to have anyone smiling at him.

Before he left people used to smile at him every day. People he knew and loved.

Once upon a time he smiled too, but something kept happening inside his head and in the end he couldn't even pretend to smile back. He felt ashamed that he could not bring himself to smile. One simple movement that didn't even have to have truth behind it, but he couldn't do it. Nobody deserved to be in the company of someone who could not even pretend to smile.

When the pain got so that it almost stopped him from breathing he used to run. He would stop on a different bridge to the one he sat beneath now and would let his fingers grip the railings as he faced the water below. Death-like stillness disturbed by tears he could not control. Always the same questions: what was wrong with him, why was he being so weak, he had a good life so why could his eyes only see in black?

He spent hours willing the river below to throw him even one answer from its watery grip. It never came.

He was alone in his soul, the loneliest place in the world.

He wasn't on his own, he had people surrounding his heart, but they couldn't get inside. They kept banging on it, his heart, like banging on a door that does not get answered though you know there is someone inside. He even gave them a key, he wanted to let them in but something inside kept blocking the way, something seemed to be piling furniture against the door.

See the doctor. Take some pills. It's not your fault. Let us help. Get through it together. Holiday. Time. Love. Patience. Break. They tried it all and he could see how much pain and worry he was causing just by being there. They didn't deserve it.

These people who tried so hard to break down the barriers of his heart, to let the sun in and watch as it gave him life did not deserve to be burdened by someone who could not even pretend to smile at the love they gave so selflessly, with nothing in return. No one deserved that. So he left.

And now he was here. Shivering in the undergrowth of existence. He didn't know if anyone was looking for him but they would be better off if they didn't. They *will* be better off if they just *forget*.

He didn't deserve a smile but he hoped the nice lady came soon. He wanted her to smile at him, to make him feel almost alive. One last time.

*

The nice lady didn't come. God's way of telling him he didn't deserve it. He didn't deserve one last smile.

*

She forgot her trainers. Her brain doesn't concentrate when she wakes up too late for breakfast. And now

95

she has to walk home in these stupid shoes. She must have left them in the car when he dropped her off in a rush this morning. Stupid shoes. She's not taking them off. Not because it's too cold, which it is, but there is no way she is walking barefoot under the bridge. It reeks of urine, so she's fairly certain this is a result of it being *steeped* in urine. No way. She'll just have to suffer.

She notices Jimmy's guitar resting against the bridge, in the spot where he usually sits. Legs crossed, head down, cradling his baby. She's quite sure his name isn't Jimmy but she sometimes hears people shout it, and it's how she thinks of him.

His pathetically thin sleeping bag lies crumpled underneath and she finds herself wondering where he is. She has walked past him most mornings and evenings going to and from work for the past week or two. Not long.

He barely even looks in her direction, as if he might be scared of human contact, of making a connection with someone, even if it is only for a second. He always looks so sad, and she always smiles. He probably doesn't notice.

Not once has she heard him play that guitar. There aren't even enough strings on it.

Jimmy Strummer, that's what they call him. Jimmy Strummer.

She hopes he isn't there because he's got shelter somewhere for the winter. Maybe whatever blip he was going through in his life is over now. She hopes so.

She smiles at the guitar that sits silently in his place. She hopes that wherever he is, Jimmy Strummer, he's at least strumming a better guitar.

REBORN
Mary Markstrom

"Oh not again!" I muttered to myself as I neared the house. "Don't tell me she's gone AWOL again."

The rusty hinges of the front door creaked, as a gust of wind caught it, dragging it over the icy step. The Yale key was still in its double lock and the translucent footprints on the slippery path had already frozen over.

Although all the signs told me she was long gone, I searched the house calling out "Mabel, it's Jessica, your carer. I've come to put you to bed."

No answer. I was getting a little bit narked. I looked my watch. I was already running late. Mabel was last on my list and I'd promised Jason I'd meet him for a couple of jars down the Crown when I finished. 'Not much hope of that now,' I thought as I went to look for Mabel.

I headed for the former Marine Docks, now converted into shops and cafes. I knew that was where her wandering feet usually carried her, and sure enough, there she was.

She was clutching a tattered canvas bag of old photographs and bits and bobs she always lugged around with her. The buttons of her grey and black mohair coat were in the wrong holes, catching it up at one end, showing the frayed hem of her flannelette nightie and the scabs on her knees from the most recent tumble she'd taken. She had a soggy blue slipper on one foot and a red canvas sneaker on the other, the untied laces trailing behind, as she squelched along the slushy pavement, searching the blank faces among the hectic throng of shoppers scurrying around her.

What did she hope to find in those unreadable features? Something; anything to connect her to the past perhaps, and her long lost child, Sophie.

Some forty odd years ago, before I was born, the adolescent Sophie had been swept into the sea by a freak wave, somewhere around where the Pizza Hut now stands.

The rescue services failed to recover Sophie's body, and Mabel's denial kept her in a time warp of constant searching and expectation. The death of her husband some years after Sophie, and the fading hopes over the decades of finding her only child, started her gradual decline into forgetfulness and wandering.

My supervisor was forever bending the ear of the social worker about residential care for Mabel, but it was always the same story, 'lack of resources.'

"You mustn't take off by yourself like this, Sweetheart." I took Mabel gently by the elbow, while sneaking a peek at my watch and thinking of Jason, waiting for me down the Crown.

"Where are you taking me?" Mabel looked alarmed.

"I have to get you home to bed now." I pointed her in the direction of my old, clapped out, red Lada or, as Jason liked to call it, my 'Stalin's Revenge.'

"Man on the telly says we can look forward to more snow tonight." I shivered and glanced at the sky.

"But, I have to meet my Sophie from school." She tried to wriggle out of my grip.

"Don't worry. We'll collect her in my car." I creaked open the passenger door for her.

"Oh, that's very sweet of you." She clambered into the car without any more fuss.

What if I had told Mabel the truth about Sophie? She'd probably have got herself all in a tizzy and I'd have had the devil of a job getting her into my car. For me, it was easier to go along with her delusions and I just didn't have time to argue.

Once she was buckled into the seat, I was relieved that she didn't mention Sophie again, that is, at least not until we were inside her house.

"Oh what a lovely home you have, Sophie!" She was gazing around like a child in Disneyland.

"This is *your* house Mabel. You've been living here for donkey's years." I helped her off with her coat. "How many times do I have to tell you? I'm *not* Sophie, I'm Jessica." This seemed to jolt her back to reality and she started to cry. I put my arms around her frail body and gave her a hug, biting my tongue for my harsh words and my impatience with her.

"Oh dear." Her bottom lip, purple with cold, began to quiver. "I get so muddled at times."

"Come on. I'll give you a nice bath and make you feel better," I said softly.

"You're so kind to me," she said through her sobs. "And I'm such a silly old woman."

Once she was bathed and ready for bed, I sat her in her greasy old, overstuffed armchair in front of the gas fire.

"Do you have children?" A fragile smile turned up the corners of her mouth.

"Nope. Footloose and fancy free, that's me. Mind you, that Jason." I rolled my eyes to the ceiling. "Worse than an overgrown kid he is at times."

This made her giggle.

"That's better. Great to see you smile." I wrapped her favourite, 'granny square' crocheted blanket around her knees. "You sit there, and I'll go and make your supper."

As I struggled to light the antiquated gas stove, my mobile throbbed in my pocket.

'When r u coming?' It was a text from Jason.

"In a bit,' I replied.

When I brought in the food tray, Mabel was sitting on the edge of her chair gazing at an old, black and white snapshot from the bag she'd been carting around. The photo was of a lanky teenager wearing a Mary Quant type mini-skirt and knee-high boots. She was peeking out from behind a curtain of

Twiggy styled hair. Mabel was repeating, 'Sophie,' quietly to herself as she studied the image, as if she was trying to make the name stick in her mind.

I took the photo from her trembling hands and settled her back into her chair. Kneeling beside her, I stroked her cold hand until she relaxed and past anxieties seemed to melt from her mind.

"Now you eat your supper while it's still hot," I nodded encouragement, but I could see she had no appetite, as she sat staring into the fire, while fidgeting with the lace of her bed-jacket.

"Aren't you eating anything, Sophie?" she looked up at me.

"I've already eaten." I dipped a piece of soft white bread into the thin chicken broth and held it out to her. Suddenly, she leaned back and glared at me with her eyes becoming big and round. It was as if she was seeing me for the first time.

"But, you're not my Sophie," she shoved the mushy bread away, sending great dollops of the stuff flying all over the place, and turned away from me with tears rolling down her cheeks. I couldn't seem to give her any sort of comfort so I went and cleaned up in the kitchen, leaving her to struggle with her torment over her long dead child, who only existed inside her head. A few faded photographs were all she had to prove that Sophie had ever existed.

'W8 4 me," I text Jason. 'B with u soon.'

When I returned to Mabel, she looked at me with tired eyes, her earlier outburst forgotten and I took her upstairs to her bedroom.

"Are you going to bed as well?" she asked as I helped her off with her slippers.

"No, I'm meeting Jason later." I looked at my watch. "I'm afraid I won't see my bed for some time." Talk of the devil. As I helped her into her rickety old, metal-framed bed, my bleeping phone told me Jason's patience was running out.

"I expect Sophie'll be home soon," Mabel whispered as I planted a goodnight peck on her pallid cheek. I swaddled her up securely in her moth-eaten candlewick counterpane in the hope that she would stay there, at least till daylight.

"I'll be back tomorrow, and don't you go wandering out in the cold again." I was aware that I sounded like a school teacher.

"Oh, I'd never do a thing like that," she chuckled as I closed the bedroom door. I made a mental note to remind my supervisor to get onto the social worker again about residential care.

When I finally reached the Crown, it was no surprise to me that Jason wasn't there. He'd probably got hacked off waiting and gone off with some of his mates, leaving me to drive home alone in my 'toxic bomb' rust bucket on wheels, with Eric Clapton singing Tears in Heaven, my favourite CD.

I set my electric blanket so high you could've fried eggs on it and cocooned myself in my hollow-fibre duvet, trying to blot out the biting cold and the racket of the wind pelting great lumps of hail against the frosted window panes. Images of Mabel tramping the streets, cold, wet and disorientated, searching for her long lost child, made me restless and put paid to any chance I had of getting too much shuteye.

"The number one rule in this job is never to become emotionally involved," the voice of my supervisor replayed in my head. "Always maintain a professional distance."

Was I becoming too involved with Mabel? My head throbbed. It's not like me at all. I have to get a grip on myself. Maybe I should ask for a change of carer for her. A dreamless, trance-like state slowly crept over me.

I woke up next day with my sweaty hair plastered over the sopping wet pillow and my ears buzzing with the sound of the phone. I peeled myself off the steaming electric blanket and slid out into the chill air. Scrubbing the grittiness out of my sleep-deprived eyes with my balled-up fist, I squinted at the flickering, eerie green figures on the radio alarm clock. No, it can't be midday. Had I forgotten to set the alarm? Relieved that I was working a late shift, I answered the phone.

"You can cross Mabel off your list for tonight." My supervisor's words made my stomach knot up.

A road cleaner had swept around a heap of rags, rigid with frost, on the pavement outside of Pound Stretcher, before realising it was a human being. While I had been wrestling with the sleep demon in my snug divan bed, Mabel had collapsed, frozen and alone in the street. How long had she lain there, cold and helpless? Nobody knew.

As I heaved open the heavy oak door of the Crown that night after work, I was happy to see Jason's cheeky grin.

"What happened to you last night?" He licked the beer froth from his moustache, and rustled a bag of BBQ Beef Hoola Hoops in my face, as I climbed onto the barstool beside him.

"It's a long story." I decorated my fingers with the little potato rings from the bag and giggled at the tickling of Jason's moustache as he gently nibbled them off.

"Never mind." He gave me a bear hug. "You're here now, so let's enjoy."

We later lay on Jason's purple Japanese futon, sipping Liebfraumilch. Jason kissed my tears away humming from *Tears from Heaven*. Time can break your heart. He knew it always made me cry but I was thinking of a girl whom I never met.

Mabel was treated in hospital for hypothermia and social workers found her a place in Sunny Bank: the best Residential Home in the area.

Jason and I often visited her there and, most of the time, she got our names right.

Tears ran down her cheeks when, almost one year later, we placed Sophie, our first born in her arms.

HONEY COTTAGE
Janet Hunt

The cottage stood all by itself, in its own country lane. Briers and honeysuckle tumbled through the hedgerows, the bees busily collecting the pollen.

An old Ford car pulled up in front of the little wicket gate, the scent of the climbing roses around the front porch sending out a welcoming greeting.

A good-looking, but tired young woman got out of the car. She took the hand of a small boy as they both gazed at the cottage with sheer joy on their faces. Simultaneously, they turned to the elderly, bespectacled man who had driven them there. The estate-agent smiled back with trepidation. He remembered how many other people had looked at the cottage with just that same look, intent on staying there for years, but only staying for a few weeks. Some had left within a few days.

He particularly recalled the little family whose first comments had been about the cluster of bee-hives at one side of the garden.

"They will have to be removed," the father of the group had announced. "And of course, I shall have to commute here every weekend."

Josh and his mother entered through the gate, followed by Mr Potts, the estate agent.

"Oh!" cried Josh's mother. "It's just beautiful." She ruffled her son's unruly hair. "I do hope that we can afford it with the money your father left us."

"H'm," said Mr Potts. "Let's just see what you think when we get inside."

"Why, it's furnished too . . . How lovely," the young woman exclaimed as she began a thorough inspection of the interior.

At the side of garden, the bees were making agitated reports to the Queen bee.

"What? Another family to be sent away?" she cried. "Call in all the workers. It's time for a council of war."

Two weeks later, Josh and his mother moved in. For a while, all was well as the little family settled in and made themselves at home.

One morning, Josh's mother was cleaning the bedroom windows when a large bee landed on her duster. It sat there fluttering its wings, intent on one thing only: to get itself onto the top of the hand which held the duster. It ruffled the hairs on its back and got ready with its sting.

May looked down and noticed him. "Oh you poor thing," she whispered. "Let me help you. I'm sure you need to be outside gathering pollen."

Gently laying down the duster, she raised the window.

"Out you go, little friend," she urged. "I do so love the honey that you little creatures make." As the bee made a bee-line for the nearest hive, she smiled to herself.

The bee arrived back at the hive in a very perplexed state. He described what had happened at the cottage. The woman was different to any of the humans that he'd ever come in contact with before.

"Nonsense," said one of the older workers. "Humans do not like us and we don't like them."

The bee then reported to the Queen.

"So the woman was kind to you.,." she said. "That changes nothing. It's the young humans that are the greatest danger to us. The campaign to get them out must continue."

Josh loved nothing more than to wander down the garden path, watching the bees hovering about the roses. One day, he stopped dead. He had almost stepped on a large bee who was so laden with pollen that it couldn't get off the ground.

"Hello," said Josh. "You seem to be in trouble."

The bee just sat there, frightened. The foot looked very big to him. Then a piece of twig was slid under him. Lifted up towards the hive, he was allowed to crawl onto the air-strip.

The hive was in a turmoil. "What shall we do?" the worker bees asked of the Queen.

"I think we should let them stay a while longer," announced the Queen, "and see how it goes."

The days drifted pleasantly by, and falling leaves signified that Autumn had arrived. It was a very wet Autumn too. One day, Josh got caught in a heavy downpour. And a couple of days later, he was so feverish that his mother sent for the doctor. However, the busy man said that there was no need to fuss, and that it was only a chill.

But it wasn't. Josh gradually got worse and the doctor was called back.

"I'm afraid it's pneumonia," the doctor announced. "But he's too ill to move. I'll call back tomorrow."

May sat up all night with Josh sponging his brow and listening to his ramblings. He wouldn't take drink or nourishment and May felt very alone.

But she wasn't.

Several of the bees had taken up residence on the top of the curtain pelmet, just as worried as May was about their friend.

The doctor returned and went away again. He came back again at tea-time.

"I'm afraid I don't hold out much hope if he doesn't get some food, or at least some liquid, down him. And he's far too ill to be moved to hospital."

The bees flew back to the hive and told the Queen what they had heard. She looked at the cells where her many baby grubs were being cradled.

"We can do for Josh, what we do for them," she announced finally.

That night, the bees got into the cottage through the usual air-brick.

May sat slumped in a chair, with her head resting on her chest. She was fast asleep.

Josh lay back on his pillow. His lips were slightly parted. The bees began to drizzle their honey into his mouth, a little at a time.

When the doctor arrived the next morning, he feared the worst. But to his amazement, Josh was sitting up in bed and looking much better.

Every night after that, the bees took turns at bringing honey for their friend. After two weeks had passed, Josh was allowed to go downstairs.

"It's a miracle," exclaimed the doctor as he closed his black bag with a smile.

With the winter came heavy snow. The bees had settled down to hibernate, so May threw some old sacks over the hive to keep the worst of the weather away. As Christmas approached, May laid in just enough food for the two of them.

However, on Christmas Eve morning there came a resounding knock on the front door. Goodness, thought May, I bet that's wrecked the holly wreath that I just hung there. When she saw who it was, she took a step backwards. Her husband's sister stood there, thin faced, her lips sucked-in so tight that you would have thought that she'd been sucking a lemon.

"Why, Maud," May said. "What a surprise. Come in won't you? I'll put the kettle on."

"Don't bother!" snapped Maud. "I'm not stopping."

Why did May feel such a sense of dread? Maud had never approved of May marrying her brother Edward.

Josh picked that moment to burst in from making a snowman in the garden.

He was the image of Edward, with the same mop of strikingly blonde hair. But somehow, this made Maud's mouth pinch even tighter.

"Well!" she said. "It's no use shilly-shallying. I've come to tell you that there'll be no more money coming to you."

May had always been pale, but now she lost what colour she might have once had.

"What do you mean Maud?" she asked, before turning to her son. "Josh! I think you'd better go to your room."

Maud sniffed loudly. "Edward's bonds have crashed," she said, "so there's no more income to come to you."

"But how are we going to live?" wailed May.

"That's *your* worry," Maud said as she turned towards the door. "Well I must be going. My train leaves in three-quarters of an hour and the taxi is waiting."

With that, she left.

In a daze, May moved over to the settee and flopped down.

"What *are* we to do?" she sighed. "What little savings we have will be gone by the Spring. We shall have to leave you," she said, looking round the gaily-decorated room.

As Christmas went by, May tried to put on a brave face for her son. Although she was being so careful with the money, it was dwindling away fast. Alone in the cold little kitchen, she spread a couple of scones with honey – honey that she'd taken from a hive.

Deep in that hive, the warmth of the spring sun awoke several of the surviving bees. As they fluttered their wings, scents from the garden were enough to rouse the rest of the hive from their slumbers. Hungry from their long fast, they were soon buzzing round the flowers. Suddenly, they remembered their friends in the cottage. It was time to pay them a visit.

"What's going on?" said one of the bees. 'Why are all these boxes being packed up?"

By eavesdropping, they soon learned what had been happening.

Back at the hive, they craved an audience with the Queen. After reporting what they had learned, the chief spokes-bee finished off with, "We've got to do something to help them, Ma'am."

After turning around several times, she announced: "Our honey has helped them before; it will surely do so again!"

Next day, the bees waited for a little white van to appear round the corner. The grocer, unaware of what was about to happen, was singing to himself. Suddenly, a swarm of bees flew in through a side-window. In panic, he tried to brush the bees away with one hand, wrenching on the steering-wheel with the other, and stamping hard on the brake pedal. As the van came to rest beside the cottage, he jumped out and made a dash for its front door. The door opened and there stood May.

"Are you all right?" she asked. "I saw what happened. My, you look upset. Do come into the kitchen. I've just made some tea."

The grocer, badly shaken, agreed. "Where did them pesky bees come from?" he said.

"I've just made some scones," May said as she made the grocer comfortable at her table. "Would you like some? There's some of my own honey too, to go with them."

Gratefully, the grocer took a bite at one of the scones. It was still warm.

"Oh!" he said, spluttering crumbs all over the table cloth. "This is so tasty. And the honey is superb. Did you say that it's your own?"

When May nodded, he held up the jar to study its amber-coloured contents. "Could you supply my shop with a few of these? I'll give you a good price."

"Certainly," said May, smiling. "I've got plenty in the back room."

In six months, May had made enough money from the sale of the honey to buy the cottage outright. It was selling so well that May had to take on staff to help her with the orders.

"Whoever would have thought that my honey would be so popular?" she chuckled as the grocer strolled into her kitchen.

"I would!" replied the grocer. "In fact, I've had a large order from abroad. Have you got the next load ready?"

"Of course I have, darling...but I'll have to leave that to the workers." She smiled coyly. "*We* shall be on our honeymoon."

As the news got round the hive, the bees buzzed happily around their Queen. Thanks to her, everything had turned out right...in the end.

BREAKING WINGS

Nancy Cook

I hear the gulls, their bold screeches like swatches of color paint-brushed across the stillness. I hear them, hear every random, shrill note, so harsh and out of tune with every other solitary screech. There are so many, all crying together and out of turn. The trails of voices cross, each voice isolated, disregarded, damning. Don't you hear me? cries one. Don't you hear me? cries another.

"They remind me of David's parents," Clare, my sister, said last summer. "The way they shriek all the time." She was visiting with her kids, Lisa and Ashley, who were at that moment throwing leftover fries at the horde of gulls crowding the deck. Our own parents never fought; at least we never heard them. Clare and I used to marvel at this, but now we understand. We both fight with our husbands, but our weapon of choice is silence.

Clare had driven in the summer heat, a straight shot on I-70, from St. Louis, where we grew up. I'm the one who refused to stay. I still go back, though, more often than I intended. I went back once already this year, in September. But I didn't drive; I flew.

In July, we talked about Christmas, Clare and I. We've always been together on Christmas, but this year, I told Clare, I might not make it. "Ben thinks we should go someplace special. To the Bahamas, maybe." Clare looked at the beach adjoining our bayfront yard and noted the irony that, of traveling a thousand miles to lie on the sand. She laughed. "Wouldn't he miss the ritual of sitting on the landing, waiting for Dad to light up the tree and tell us it's okay, Santa made it all right?"

I looked away. In the sky were clouds like threads of egg white; the blue over the bay was that pallid color, like faded muslin. I thought of home. "It isn't just Ben," I said. "It's me. It feels phony. It's being treated like children still, when we're not. Ashley and Lisa are the children now."

If Clare understood, she didn't say. She reminded me that Mom and Dad were getting older, too.

Autumn's desolation envelops the beach. The bay steals up the strand, reaching for the marsh grass and sweeping it clean of small impressions: crabs' claws, tiny shells, sandpipers' prints. A goose, grey and brown, stands a few yards from the water's edge. She's been there, motionless, forlorn, for three days now. At dusk, when the flocks pass overhead, their jumbled voices teeming like the barking of dogs, I think of her. I wonder if she will leave her lonely post and join them. As the November sun dissipates, she fades from my sight. But it doesn't matter; I know. I know she will not fly with the others.

Geese mate for life. My father told me this. If one has been struck by a hunter's gun, or has lost the way, the mate, the life's partner, will wait. I wonder if the geese understand about broken hearts; or do they speak of broken wings?

My mother met me when I got off the plane in St. Louis that September day. Lisa and Ashley were with her. We spoke only of small things, and told ourselves it was for the sake of the girls. Back at the house, Ashley and Lisa played dress-up. Lisa wore my father's old fedora and worn-out penny loafers. Ashley was content to wear my sister's First Communion veil and my mother's pink slippers until she noticed the pennies in the loafers. She wanted the shoes with money in them, and when Lisa declined to trade, Ashley tried to hit her. My mother intervened by grasping Ashley's hand. Lisa screamed in anger, and first Ashley started to cry, then Lisa. My mother knelt, taking both girls in her arms, and my mother, too, cried.

I didn't cry, and I made no move to comfort my mother.

I sense the movement of wings, a flock uniting, a huge dark blur waxing in the cold light. They are behind me, in the fields, these strong-winged birds:

Canada geese the color of the landscape, Snow geese like great puffed oysters, invading the quiet with their flight. They come here to feed, to claim what the farmers have left behind, to take their rest before continuing on the long, nomadic, skyward migration.

In my father's den are pictures of these geese, and of other birds, replications of paintings done by Audubon in the late nineteenth century. I have read stories of Audubon, a man who, for the love of science or art, or perhaps simply for the momentary thrill of conquest, captured and killed each living, beautiful bird he studied; how with knives he was thus able to achieve his formidable knowledge and stunning artistic accuracy.

I never told anyone what I knew. There were phone calls on late afternoons, with the sounds of my mother's hushed, happy murmurings and her foot brushing the polished pinewood floorboards, coursing like soft rain and distant thunder through the house. There was a man once or twice, taller than my father, with too black hair, a stiff dark suit, and a husky laugh. I was ten, and always first to get home from school. But for a while, until it was over, I eased my pace. I stepped on every sidewalk crack, and hoped Clare wouldn't see.

Then it was done and we were a family again, with never a trace of the man who might have destroyed us. Over nightly dinners, while Clare and I talked of school and friends, our father punctuated the conversations with his jokes and his small teasing touches to our cheeks and ears, and our mother kept her silent watch over the table. I went along. But when I could, I moved thousands of miles so that I would not speak of it, the thing I knew.

Winter is coming early this year. Unlike summer, with its storms that can be seen for miles, approaching through the bold rustle of leaves, spreading red and purple light like ink across the water, winter slips in unseen and unheard, late at night. It silences the bay, and dispossesses the birds. Tonight, or tomorrow night, the bay will freeze, locking in the life below. The gulls will cry, and search the solid stillness for a rift; but they will move on, to find refuge in another place.

And when the bay freezes, and the waves no longer lap the shore; when the migrant geese are gone, their beating wings and barking songs no longer the music of our darkened existence, then the silence will enter my dreams, disturb the gentle tide of sleep, and wake me. If I rise, and go into the living room, where the big glass doors, icy from the flying spray, come between me and the black emptiness outside; if I go there, and wait for the fear to pass, I wonder if I will wait alone, or if the solitary goose who occupies the beach will keep watch with me.

The phone that rang in the middle of the September night could carry only one kind of message. But when Clare told me that our father had suffered a stroke and was in a coma, I was foolish enough to hope. I thought we could do something; I wanted to break through the ice.

But he died. And after he died, after the funeral, when I returned to this remote shore country, I saw only loneliness in its flat, brown-and-green sameness. I heard the cold in the beating of wings, and in the sharp voices of the gulls.

Last night I dreamed of returning to my childhood home. It was windy and snowing as I mounted the front porch steps. I was sad because I knew someone would not be there, someone I loved, someone who should be there. But more than sad, I was afraid. I had no gift for my mother, as I thought I should, and I knew that her disappointment would pain her.

In the dream, my father met me at the door. He reached out to enclose me in a warmth of flannel and wool; and as I breathed in the comfort of his old clothes, I heard his voice, soft as down, "Don't worry, don't worry now; everything will be all right."

I can no longer hear the gulls. They have disappeared with the whitewashed sun. I have only the waves to keep me company for this little while, until Ben comes home. But maybe that is enough. The rhythmic throbbing that rocks the desolate shore can cradle the heart as well; perhaps it even has the power to heal broken wings.

WHISPER MY NAME
Arleen Freeman

Very late afternoon. Weak dappled winter sunshine peeps through the wrinkled and withered trees that cling to forest coloured banks. Moss crawls over rough roadside rocks and decaying umber leaves spill across the edges, whilst wet winter grasses curtsey on hard, blackened turf. Along the path side the silent stream does not meander and sing summers song, for now she is frozen and mercurial in her beauty.

The birdsong has also fled this ancient landscape which has given way to the desolate cold. Winter hums the tune of darkness, death and destruction as he tightens his steely grip on Mother Earth. She who sleeps under a moonstone blanket, sighing for summer warmth, but like a jealous lover, winter guards the Earth wrapping her in the cords of the wind. Until Earth gives up her smell of damp, dense, decay and the air is peppered with smoky wood burning chimneys from the few stone farmhouses living in this valley.

Into this bleak winter world I cycle avoiding pitted potholes of an uncared for country lane. My breath comes out in small white puffs in the growing mists that creep along the valley. Glad of my winter coat, my bike groans in protest under the weight of my suitcase. I can clearly see the old rustic farmhouse nestled on the land, wooded trees at its back doorstep. I imagine my warm welcome by fireside.

Sighing dreamily I think of my love, Emile, tall, dark, traditionally handsome waiting for me, as well as his Mama, honest and homely. She who has nurtured me since coming to this land.

Happily I pedal faster and faster until I enter the farmyard, just ahead of the cold winter twilight. Animals are bedding down for the night as I dismount. Entering into the cosy kitchen, I discard my coat as Mama envelopes me, placing her apron over my head, a sign of my homecoming. Extending my hands to the fires warmth I sink into the old overstuffed armchair. Mama gives me my tea, then takes my precious suitcase to the bedroom.

Hungrily I devour my steaming vegetable soup and coarse brown bread, thankful for a warm meal in harsh winter times. For my work is very intense and I feel the hunger as I pedal on and on, never knowing where I'll lay my head at night. Yet this family is my safe home in winter storms. Gradually I begin to relax, I'm so tired, my eyelids droop, where is Emile I wonder, where is my love?

Unexpectedly I hear gunshot, immediately drowsiness flees, Mama! I rush along the familiar dark passageway, my breathing coming in shallow, frightened gasps. And there in the candlelight, is Mama, her body slumped over. Stifling a scream I kneel and touch her. I can smell the sticky, sweet stench of her blood as it pools on the winter slate flooring. Shakily I stand up. I feel sick. She is dead! I can't look, can't think, can't move! I stare down in horror at my bloodied hands. I can't breathe, "Emile, Emile," I cry out!

Hastily I retreat down night's passageway, stumbling into the kitchen, wiping my bloodied hands down Mama's apron. I hear the dying groans of the intruder. "Emile", I gasp. I smell him before I see him, smoking, sensual, steady-eyed, grimly bent to the task of reloading. "Mama's dead!" I cry out. In one swift stride Emile crosses the kitchen floor and fiercely hugs me. He can't speak.

Realising the urgency of our situation I sweep brown bread and cheese from the gnarled oak table into a cotton pillowslip. Determinedly I walk to the wall, rough plaster scrapes my fingers as I wrench Mama's photo from its hook.

Flinging on my winter coat I blindly look for my suitcase "I got it from..." and Emile points to the dead intruder. "We must go now, must leave!" Emile rasps out.

"Mama", I choke on her name tasting hot, salty tears. I couldn't save her instead I touched the hand of death and it was deep and dark and dank. "I love you", Emile whispers my name. Then he takes my cold, trembling arm. "Time to leave"

"Someone's pounding on the door Emile!"

"Back way" he mouths, handing me my suitcase whilst he holds his gun aloft a cold, hard expression crossing his face.

Together, rushing to the back door. "Bang!" Emile crumples against the heavy wooden frame. This lands intruders force me to my knees, a cold steel message slides down the side of my head. My facial bones ache, I clutch my suitcase. Winter enters my heart, my love lies on a cold stone floor. A life so precious to me...Seconds tick by...

Suddenly a violent blast rips through the farmhouse. Stone shatters, intruders scream, deaths scythe is busy. Through the choking dust, miraculously Emile is on his feet, eyes like flint, pulling me up and through the back door to freedom.

My mind can't grasp he's alive, my love is alive! Then running, running into the bitter, biting cold, my suitcase safe with its secret portal ready to connect to

London. Emile whispers my name, my eyes fill with tears for I now know winter is wars darkness, crawling into the deep shadows of the Earth, relentlessly seeking an English wireless operator.

Very early evening, France 1942.

THE DOG
Mel Hague

Oddbod pulled the flap down and peered into the gloom, he could make out the frost covered scrub and the junk that littered the area, the low mist overlaying the ground and a bus going by in the distance. '*Much too early,*' he thought and pushed the flap back into place. He snuggled down into the raggedy, old sleeping bag and tried to drop off but it was just too cold. He'd been living rough now for several years and he'd managed to find three boxes that fit neatly inside each other with a good thickness of newspapers between each to give him a three layer, insulated cardboard home which managed to stave off hyperthermia each winter but this winter was the worst he'd ever known. Two tramps and a bag lady had died in the last few days and Oddbod expected a few more would succumb in the coming days if the temperature didn't rise above freezing soon.

An hour later he peered out again but although the sky was lighter the frost was keener and the mist much denser so he pushed the flap back in place and snuggled down again but he would have to make a move soon as his stomach was beginning to gripe. He pulled the sleeping bag over his head and then his box was shaken by something heavy and a deep growl followed by a fierce bark which terrified him into retreating to the back of his cardboard home. The barking continued for several minutes then stopped suddenly. He crept forward and pulled down the flap and saw a large dog blending into the mist in the distance. No-one else was about but he went along the viaduct tapping on the boxes and lean-to's to ask if they'd heard the big dog barking but the few who were still 'at home' said they'd heard nothing.

It happened again the next morning and the morning after that and still the freezing weather persisted; it was mind-numbingly cold and Oddbod feared he would freeze to death while he slept just like the bag lady he'd spoken to a couple of days ago. He put it from his mind as he made his rounds but the streets were deserted so he was reduced to scratching about in rubbish bins for scraps of food and as he crawled into his box that night he began to worry; he'd eaten so little in the last few days and yet he wasn't really hungry. Was he going into a state of near-death?

All through the night he heard the dog whining and howling while he struggled to sleep. Daylight took ages to come through the heavy mist and Oddbod wondered how the normal folks were coping with the sub-zero temperatures and the dense misty fog. It must be playing havoc with their cars and plumbing. He remembered the times when he'd had a proper house with plumbing and central heating and a cozy gas fire with a two-tone pink Vauxhall Cresta in the garage. He loved that car but nothing lasts forever, especially cars. The dog crashed into his box/home again and barked fit to wake the dead. After a few minutes it stopped and as Oddbod peered out over the flap he saw the beast blending into the mist and then it was gone.

He unravelled the greatcoat from his sleeping bag and crawled out to meet the day but there wasn't much to see. A thick coat of ankle-deep snow had fallen during the night and everything was brilliant white from the edge of his box to the heavy mist barely twenty yards away. Oddbod pulled on his woollen gloves and took a steady walk under the huge viaduct to check on his neighbours. Two more had died during the night; an old timer in his seventies and a young feller who'd only been here a couple of weeks. That surprised him, it was usually the old 'uns who died in a harsh winter but then the young man didn't have much meat on his bones so he probably couldn't generate enough body heat to stave off the severe cold.

Oddbod was in his late forties and had a bit of a middle-age spread. He patted his stomach and thanked his lucky stars that he ate well enough to keep an ample amount of fat on his body to stay alive. As he walked along he noticed that the boxes were all empty apart from the ones containing the corpses. He couldn't recall hearing anyone knocking about and it was certainly unusual for everyone to leave the site at the same time. Street folk were very possessive of their meagre belongings and their shelters so it was generally accepted that a few would stay behind to keep an eye on things and the ones who left to forage would try to beg enough food and money to bring something back for the watchers. *'But, of course,'* he thought, *'I'm here and these two stiffs who they probably assumed were still alive.'* He walked back to his box and crawled in to wait for the others to bring home the goodies.

When he awoke again it was dark and nothing had been pushed through his flap so the miserable sods hadn't brought anything back for him. Well if that's the way they wanted to be then he would be up early in the morning and off into the town to his more profitable spots and everything he brought back would be for himself. *'Bugger 'em,'* he thought and started to drift back off to sleep but another thought crossed his mind, *"I'll share with the young lad, he's not been at it long enough to get streetwise.'* He was pulling the sleeping bag over his head when he remembered the lad was dead, he'd found him frozen stiff in his box just this morning. He heaved a sigh and then snuggled down for the night.

Deep sleep had barely claimed him before the dog struck up again with his barking and howling and it persisted 'til just before daylight when it rounded off its disturbance by bashing his box and barking so loud that Oddbod knew it was just the other side of his flap. He decided that he couldn't take any more of this harassment and as soon as it was light he would scour the immediate area for something long enough and hard enough to kill that damned dog before it drove him mad.

With the gravity of exhaustion pulling at his weary body he crawled out of his box as the dawn broke and stepped into the fresh snow that had fallen overnight again and peered into the even thicker mist which was much closer than yesterday. How he was going to find anything to beat the dog with in this deeper snow and heavier mist he couldn't begin to comprehend but he was sure as hell going to try. He had to. He couldn't take another night like these last few.

Keeping the weak glow of the morning sun directly ahead he walked on, testing the ground with his feet for dangerous holes or debris and anything remotely resembling a club. He found nothing; and when he turned around he could see nothing and a shudder of panic crept up his body.

"What have you done, you silly bugger?" he said aloud, "you've gone and got yourself lost, that's what you've done." He took a few tentative steps forward. "You could freeze to death out here in this snow and nobody would find you for days, maybe weeks." He looked back and tried to align himself with the watery glow of the sun and with mounting trepidation he turned forward and walked on hoping he would make it back to the viaduct. The top of the viaduct was a hundred feet above the ground but it was nowhere in sight; the mist was not only dense but it was very deep so he had no landmark to guide him home.

Looking about he tried to retrace his steps but he couldn't find them and he decided that he must have drifted too far to one side or the other of the footprints he'd made on his way out. Stumbling along in deep despair he felt tears beginning to fill his eyes and wiped them away; they would freeze in these temperatures and then he wouldn't be able to see anything. He'd wandered out too far and he quietly cursed himself for being so naïve. There was a price to pay for such stupidity and he was surely going to pay it. Finally he saw a dark figure and as he moved closer he recognized the police uniform and could just see the man was holding a mobile phone to his ear.

Oddbod walked past and heard him say, "That's right, Guv, six bodies frozen to death under the viaduct. I don't suppose anyone will miss 'em but I wouldn't wish that sort of death on anyone. The Coroner has brought two meat wagons and he's collecting the bodies now. Yes, Guv, will do."

"Six bodies," Oddbod said. "Someone else must have died last night. This is awful." He moved closer and saw several people standing around his precious box. "Hey! That's my box. What the hell are you doing?"

They ignored him and a plainclothes detective asked the coroner for an estimate of the time of death and he replied, "Not sure. It's difficult in this kind of weather but I'd say he's been dead for three or four days at least."

Oddbod's mouth dropped open when he saw them pull the body out of the box. He recognized the blue sleeping bag, the greatcoat and the woollen gloves. "It can't be. That's me; but I'm standing right here." Panic gripped him as he added, "There's been a mistake. An awful mistake."

Something pushed against his hand and when he looked down it was the dog. He absently stroked the fur behind its ears and then said softly, "Good grief, I'm dead." He looked down at the ground and couldn't see any paw prints in the snow and as he turned he realized that he hadn't left any footprints in the snow. The dog gripped his sleeve and gently tugged him along and they fell in step with the bag lady, the young man and the three old guys. They were all smiling and gesturing for him and the dog to lead the way.

The dog looked up at him and cocked its head to one side and Oddbod said, "I know you, you were my dog when I was a lad. I recognize the different coloured markings. My folks were going to call you Spot or Patches but I named you Oddbits. As he walked Oddbod turned and looked behind and couldn't see any prints left by either of them. He shrugged and said, "Come on then, boy, lead on." The mist began to drift away, the snow got thinner and the sun got stronger. He began to feel warm; warmer in fact than he'd felt in weeks.

First Prize

WINTERREISE
Susan Imgrund

'Aim for the moon, *bua.*'

Toni heard his father's words as he tramped upwards, through a forest frozen in dark grey. Above him, a pale and silent moon hung trapped in inky clouds. He straightened his shoulders against the dead weight of the wooden skis, inhaling the early morning air.

'Aim for the moon and someone will shoot you in the back,' Franz had muttered. Toni's older brother had prematurely aged by taking on Father's responsibilities as a boy whose voice had barely broken. Twenty-two and resigned to the drudgery of being a farmer for the rest of his days.

Toni had been greeted with a bovine snore from Franz's corner when he'd come in last night. There had still been sounds of snoring as he'd crept out an hour or two ago. Franz would be up by now, milking, mucking out, bogged down in pails and filthy straw and the reek of cow shit. Toni strode up the mountain path, chilly air in his lungs, the moon and stars in his view.

What *had* become of Father? Could it be that he, too, saw that moon, somewhere ahead? Or was he long dead, a frozen corpse amongst thousands strewn across the wastelands of Russia?

Father wouldn't have disapproved, as Franz had with his pious criticisms and slurs. Fancy ideas above your station. Work-shy. Fallen in with the wrong crowd. Toni smiled into his swirling breath and rubbed his hands as he thought back to his first sortie with Sepp Hagleitner and his gang. He'd been shit-scared. Not of the ski-ing, oh, no – he could ski rings around Sepp ten times over. His childhood friend had developed too much of a liking for beer and liver dumplings for any nimble prowess on skis.

It was the danger. Raw, incessant, unmerciful. The border patrol would not hesitate to shoot, even if a flicker of doubt remained. They must set an example. Others must be discouraged at all costs. The war had been over for six years, but this eternal battle was still being fought.

Toni felt that fear again as he headed upwards, turning off the main path onto a narrow trail used by hunters. It had been one thing playing this game with Sepp and the lads, fuelled by home-made schnapps and smutty jokes. But now he was alone with his forebodings.

Twigs scratched Toni's face as he pushed through the trees, rucksack and skis behind him. The snow on the forest floor lay pitted by drips from low branches. Somewhere in the near distance an owl called, a solemn echo, like the priest in the village chapel at Midnight Mass.

Sepp and the gang hadn't wanted to go over again before Christmas. They've got the heebie-jeebies up there, the guards, Sepp had said. They're going to have eagle eyes on top of eagle eyes this time of year. Too risky. Toni, my friend, you're better off downing a *Heimaterde* or six with the boys by the log fire in the *Schwarzer Adler* and seeing if you can't get Annelise Gruber to warm you up a little.

But Sepp had not seen little Gretl's worn-through shoes or Mama's hunger-drained cheeks.

The moon began to fade and the sky wore a tinge of pink as Toni neared the old hunters' hut. The thought of Annelise swept away the snow, the chill. They had gathered mushrooms here in September, *Pfifferlinge* and *Steinpilze*. The forest that day had been dappled with smiling sunlight, busy with the chatter of jays and squirrels.

Herr Gruber had big plans for the *Schwarzer Adler*. Already, the tourists were trickling back, like a mountain stream in the first day of thaw. The Germans, of course, a few Dutch, the odd English couple. Toni had spent last winter as a ski instructor. On these slopes that he'd known since boyhood, he'd fought a losing but good-hearted battle against limbs too set in their ways and stomachs that yearned for their fill of pork knuckle and *Sauerkraut*. He gazed ahead, where the trees ended, over the expanse of dawn-dusted snow, up towards the pass. Gruber planned to build a cable car here. And where would that put Franz and his cows and his barley broth?

Ever upwards he climbed, called by the peaks, granite and ice from a distant, glacial time. Here the trees stood in brave isolation, like sentinels. Guards. God, just give me this one chance and then it'll all be above board. I can make enough as a ski instructor once the season gets underway. Enough to get into old man Gruber's good books, enough that Annelise is proud to walk out with me, enough that I won't reek of cow for the rest of my life. But just now, for today, for the week before Christmas, I must provide where Franz cannot.

Rocks or border control? Toni peered through his binoculars at the two black shapes far across the snow, on the edge of the promised land. They hadn't moved, but...wait, one had started...

Toni laughed. He watched the mountain goat bound away out of sight. Perhaps the grass was greener over there for that rascal, too. Toni strapped on his skis and adjusted his rucksack. He traversed silently across the virgin snow, wind against his cheeks, goal within his grasp.

He slowed at the first border sign. Red-white-red. No sign of the guards – probably at the schnapps in some hunter's hut, and who could blame them? It was a bleak and thankless existence so near to Christmas. Toni poled his way upwards to the next sign. White cross on red. Only 500 metres to go, downhill – and he was going to savour it. As yet he had committed no crime.

*****

'Ah, Walser, my young Tiroler friend!' Hubertus ushered Toni into the warmth of the mountain hut. 'You could not stay away from my little Swiss paradise, I see? Well, I have much to offer... you need a new camera, perhaps?'

"Fraid I'm a bit short on cash, Hubertus, just before Christmas,' Toni hauled his rucksack onto the counter and looked into the old man's rosy face, well-fed with neutrality. 'But I can pay partly in butter, this time. I've brought as much as I could carry...'

Toni breathed in the smell of fresh coffee. The little room was indeed a paradise – cameras of the very latest design, Camel and Lucky Strike cartons stacked to the ceiling, more chocolate than he'd ever seen...

Hubertus loaded the rucksack with cigarettes and tobacco. It would be lighter on the way back than the butter, at least. Toni's eye caught sight of packs of nylon stockings. He reached for three. They would hardly weigh the rucksack down any more and might melt Annelise's recent frostiness...

'I am afraid, young Walser, that I'll need more than a few *Groschen* and Tiroler butter – excellent though it may be – for these goods. But as you are a special friend, and it is Christmas, you can come back to me with the balance in the New Year.'

'I promise, Hubertus.'

*****

Toni timed his return exactly. He had to start at dusk – dark enough to evade the border patrol but light enough to ski back down to the village. Hubertus had plied him with a good meal of cheese noodles washed down with beer and real, strong coffee. The safe warmth of the hut was extinguished as soon as he set foot outside by the unforgiving chill of the sunless afternoon. He rubbed his gloved hands together, adjusted his rucksack and threw his skis down on the fresh snow.

Part traversing, part side-stepping upwards, the way out of paradise was more gruelling than the way in. And he had to remain vigilant – if he was caught now, he was done for. Toni took a few steps, stopped, looked, listened. And another few steps. Not far now.

He'd try the way beneath the signs. Sepp had shown him last time. A band of rock provided some cover but it was a narrow traverse with a sheer drop to the right. He had to have his wits about him. Down here, and here...across...his skis slicing through the soft snow. The wind scraped his cheeks.

The visibility dimmed. What was up? What was down? He skied by instinct...

'Hey, you!' The voice came from above. Toni did not stop. Onward...just...

...the searing pain in his leg...the shot. Like a rebound. Toni collapsed. He yelled, his howls filling the mountains with their echo. His leg burned as blood seeped into the snow. Red on white...

Someone stood over him now, was shouting. Toni looked up. A rifle, a border guard. And above the rifle and the guard, in a salmon-and-ink sky, the moon.

*****

Georg Walser looks at the moon and smiles a forgotten smile. He stands above the village that he left seven years ago, to fight in a cold, eastern land. He has killed. He has starved. He has suffered. But that is the past. Down there, in a cosy parlour, he smells a wood fire, fresh hay, barley broth. There are his darling Rosa, his boys, his little Gretl.

He has come home.

WINTER 2056: FRAGMENTS
A.R. Paul

So low in the sky, the sun. Distended light spreads about us, on the horizontal. Without strength it is, stone against our skin. Though dazzling even now, because magnified by the ice-floor. I stare until my retinas are scored. In the afternoons, its light retains enough energy to bounce off the houses, and off the empty apartment blocks along the ancient north road. The walls' honey grain glows gold and pink, a cinematic show of old. I persuade myself I see the diminished sun's output fan across the permafrost like a trekking mammal seeking its breeding ground. It puts me in mind of those crude old travel posters: an array of beams from a setting sun, paradise across the ocean. Except here there's no warmth. Trudging up the hill, I stop at intervals to bask in the light, a blue lizard.

The mercury has not risen above minus ten for two months. Peters maintains a log. For posterity, he says. Someday, someone will find it. When the world has turned again, when the survivors of us emerge into temperate existence once more, his record will be the true and faithful evidence of what we lived through. Peters, I think, enjoys the morbidity of his task: he loved documenting the eighteen consecutive nights when the temperature slipped to minus forty below, a record so far. Nothing tickles him more than being able to report his measurements. We connive in his grim delight, grinning with him, but we all realise this is a mask we wear against anxiety.

Perforce, we must wrap ourselves in eight, nine, ten layers. Out in the street, we endeavour to move fast. But the cold saps our efforts. We have not yet adapted our movements to the conditions.

Here is our tragedy: we can all too clearly remember how things were. We understand what we have lost, for when it came, the freeze came quickly. The delights available to our parents dissipated in half a decade. Systems disintegrated. Distribution dried up. For a while we mourned for the automated systems, the voice-controlled doors, lights and appliances. For the thrum of ambient-modulated central heating. For hologram shopping. Until we realised that in the very convenience lay the problem.

We know of one or two people in their nineties whose lives have witnessed the entire life-cycle of risen technology and its fall. That they are coping as well as any of us speaks volumes.

The world has shrunk back to a matter of streets. For a century, people had used the word "community" and applied it to everything. Imagine: people even used the phrase "the global community". That's a fine joke now. As the extent of our viewpoint scaled back, like refocusing a telescope onto what was directly in front of us, we had to find our own community, had to redefine the word, make it meaningful again.

We are a lonely species, unaccompanied as we are by beasts of earth or air. For a few years crows thrived. Their throaty call was as present as the wind in the dead wires strung over our barren streets. They were smudges of motion, of interest, against the white backdrop. But now even they have disappeared, died off or migrated south to try their luck elsewhere. I miss their croaking racket.

For comfort, we have only one another. We live in each other's homes. Beside our fires we gather, ragged, but magnetized to one another by hope and despair in equal measure.

Our pleasures are not those of our grandparents. Nor even of our parents. We have taken to dancing. One or two amongst us have sufficient musicality to grind a tune from an old violin or untuned piano. The dances we shape from invention. They were born amidst caution and embarrassment, a fear they were nothing but parodies, simulacrae of how we thought we ought to move. Later, we forgot ourselves. We slipped the trappings of inhibition. Now, as we gyrate and sway, we ululate like Nubians. In the flame-light, the silhouettes cast by our thrown limbs tell us how it might have been to live in caves.

Our indoor lives are spent in front of the fire. We have ripped out the old gas fittings, re-opened fire-places and sent small boys up ladders to clear the tops of chimneys. Conscious of retrieving the old ways, we understood, too, we would have to learn them for ourselves. There were no manuals. No on-line tutorials.

My favourite moments are in the long hour of afternoon's twilight. I stand on the hill and watch the sun edge round before it sinks. Here is the colour in my world. Strangers will stop and watch with me. As is the way now we hold each other and silently lament. We know it is not our sun anymore. Tears as big as hailstones will fall.

Of our human relations, there is surprising evolution. It goes further than wrapping ourselves in the fire-warmth and working ourselves into a dance-frenzy. Most of us can remember a time when there were unwritten but strict rules about touch. There was a certain amount of casual hugging, it's true. But in general it had well-circumscribed boundaries. That has changed now, in the face of the relentless freeze. If our ancient ancestors of the harsh north, being frigid in their relations, withdrew from one another and retreated into small, well-defined family units, we by contrast have ventured in the contrary direction. We have become uninhibited about physicality. It is a tenet for us that the language of touch is a legitimate medium. We have developed new distinctions between sexual and non-sexual contact. When we are not dancing in front of the fire, we embrace each other for warmth and social union. It is a necessity as well as a comfort. We have become a tactile generation.

There are faint folk memories among us regarding how to manage. Practical measures excavated from our collective intelligence are carrying us through. But even we, in our make-do existence, are tempted by whim and rumour. Whenever we hear reference to some old method, some old wives' tale, we grasp it like prospectors. There was a craze for eating acorns last autumn – someone said they were rich in vitamin D and the word spread among us like that old winter vomiting bug that killed so many in the twenties and thirties.

Opening up the chimneys has been one of our best moves. They stood unused for a hundred years. Instead, highly tuned boiler-systems propelled heated water around pipes. Sensors regulated our domestic temperatures to half-degrees. A miracle of technology. Until the fuel ran out.

That's not strictly true. There is fuel out there still. There is the know-how. Great minds had worked out the methods, had developed new ways to sustain our life-style. But, in the event, the systems broke down under the weight of demand. Everyone wanted more.

And once the freeze was accepted as normality none of us imagined it would so affect our capacity to cope, our ability as humans to function. The assumption was that we would adapt and survive, that systems would be adjusted. But the cold ground us down. Only in the last few years have we started to find our feet. In the meantime, the power stations stopped running, and the networks, so it is said, are irrecoverable.

We cook over the fire. We make large pots of broth, concocted from the fragments of a recipe one of us remembered, or heard about. Or perhaps we only imagine it comes from the past. Perhaps, I prefer to think, we are innovating as we go, the thread of human ingenuity not yet frozen out.

Our world barely extends beyond a few streets. Peters goes walking now and then, across the river, or the other side of the old railway line. He brings back intelligence, some usable bric-a-brac, or – if we are lucky – food. For the most part, we speculate about what might be going on elsewhere. I find I imagine the Nubians in the new temperate zone, laying out streets and towns, car parks, bowling alleys, and coffee shops, with smiles as wide as the Nile. We sometimes talk of migrating.

Some of our number insist everything we do has its roots in the past. That the way we live is evolutionary, a natural progression. They like to say that all our new ways existed as tendencies before the new ice age. Perhaps so.

For myself, I am incurious about causes and precedents. The past let us down. Our forebears, over too many generations, took the future for granted. They talked a good talk, speaking freely about "our grandchildren", but they did not truly envision the future of those who would come after. They assumed they could have it both ways. They wanted both bread tomorrow and jam today. Our current lives are the product of that dual desire.

We know that we – our specie – have been through this before. The idea that a new phase will occur, that we will one day feel again the full warmth of the sun, provides us with a kind of faith. Yet if it is not a blind one, then it is certainly partially-sighted. For it will not, I think, happen in my lifetime; nor those of my children, nor my children's children, if, God help them, they have any. For the sake of our sanity, therefore, we must be pragmatic: we have seen the best of what the world had to offer, but we will not see it again.

We are the crows, now. The scavengers in the snow. Peters, putting a positive slant on things, calls us bricoleurs, fabricating our survival by combining remnants. Our culture, our habits, are a patchwork quilt, a hotch-potch of discards, of whatever we can make work for us. The eighteenth and nineteenth centuries were the great age of classification; the twentieth, with all its horrors, taught us to wean ourselves off the mania for labelling and easy categories. In this century, we have learnt the hard way to accept things for what they are.

I count in this my clinging to the low sun, my stopping to gaze at its effects as it passes across the ice. It is a heart, I tell Peters, a heart on go-slow, one that will perhaps, one day, beat in full time again. In the meantime, it remains an incipient beauty, yet to flower. I am happy to be dazzled by its tepid glare. I scar my retinas with the idea of possibility.

WINTER SHOES
Anita Gilson

Barney Summers left the Clave Circus School by the side door, and looked at the grey, sleety flakes of snow. It was light snow, not settling, but vanishing as it touched the pavement, and the air was warm.

Barney did a cartwheel in celebration. Today, Pepe Svarbos, who ran the Clown Classes, had given him a rare compliment.

"You have what it takes, young man," he said. "You have the gift of laughter within you. That cannot be taught. I can give you technique, teach you acrobatic skills, and how to play musical instruments. I can give you routines to perform. But the gift of laughter I cannot give you. That lives in your heart."

"Thank you, sir," Barney had said shyly, feeling his face flush with joy.

"You know what else you have?" went on the great man, who had brought laughter to generations of children and adults alike, "You have humanity. You cannot truly be a clown, without a love for your fellow human beings."

"Thank you," Barney had said again. He did another cartwheel and walked a few steps on his hands, and then collapsed, deliberately, in a comic fall.

"Still at it? Don't you ever stop?" said a voice. It was Andreas Ullanos, who had finished his trapeze class and was also on his way home.

Barney shrugged. Andreas was a fine one to talk. He was obsessive about his art. Long dark hair, huge lustrous eyes, slender and graceful, the girls swooned round him. Not like me, thought Barney who was skinny, with wild red curls and a turned up nose. Everyone treated him like a kid brother.

They walked together through the sleety streets gleaming wet like the skin of seals, heading for Caderby Gardens, where they shared digs. Barney told him what the great Pepe had said, and Andreas was impressed.

"Not often he gives out compliments," said Andreas. "You must be REALLY good."

"Don't know," Barney said, modestly. "Just hope I can keep affording the fees."

Andreas was lucky. He came from a large circus family, who all chipped in to pay his fees. Barney's widowed mother did not have that kind of money. Barney worked in a pub, a café and did cleaning to raise the cash for his own fees, and help his mum as well.

As they walked through the sleet, a young man came towards them. He had a pleasant face, a sweet smile, and silky shoulder-length hair. And the strange thing about him was that he was barefoot, treading the wet pavement without shoes or socks.

"Have you got any spare change?" he asked. "I'm saving up to buy some shoes."

Andreas laughed, somewhat disbelievingly, and gave him 50p.

"Go on then," he said, indulgently.

"Thank you," the young man's voice was musical. "Thank you. You'll go far. Rise in your profession."

"I hope so. I'm a trapeze artist." Andreas laughed.

Barney searched his pockets. He had been going to get a pizza for tea, but bread and cheese would be just as nourishing, and this young man's shoes were more important now the weather was running cold. He offered the young man a five-pound note. And hoped he'd be able to pay his rent.

"Bless you," said the barefoot man. "Bless you with diamonds."

The phrase stuck in Barney's mind for a long time afterwards.

"You gave him a fiver!" cried Andreas, "Barney, you're crazy. He's got more money than you I bet."

"Rubbish! I have shoes at least," said Barney.

Andreas shook his head. "How are you going to pay your Circus School fees, if you throw money away, like that?"

Barney sighed. Perhaps he could try for a scholarship. Pepe had told him he had talent. Maybe he stood a chance. But there would be hundreds of talented young artistes going for the two scholarships. However, the barefoot man's needs had been greater.

Three weeks later, Barney was making his way home alone. The snow was twirling thickly though still melting as it touched the grey pavement. Once again the young man came towards him. There was something beautiful about him. Such a sweet face, Barney thought, and such beautiful hair. He was still barefoot, and clearly did not remember Barney.

"Have you any spare change?" he asked. "I'm saving up to buy some shoes."

Barney stopped. Clearly he was scamming the public. But then it struck him that maybe people had not been generous to him, so he gave him five pounds again.

"Bless you," said the young man. "Bless you with diamonds."

Barney smiled. Now there was a way to raise his Circus School fees.

The young man did not appear again, and Barney was relieved. He really couldn't afford to keep shelling out fivers like this.

A month later, the weather turned bitterly cold. The sky was dark, but the sun edged the clouds and lit up everything like a magic halo. Barney came home to find Mrs Molly, his landlady, in a flutter.

"There's an official looking bloke wants to see you," she said. "What have you been up to?"

She ushered Barney into her front room. A dark-suited, middle-aged man was perched on the floral sofa, smiling beneath his dapper moustache.

"Here he is," said Mrs Molly, "I hope he's not in any trouble."

"Not at all," said the dark-suited man, smiling more than ever, "Far from it."

Mrs Molly hung about. The dark-suited man cleared his throat discretely, and she flounced out. Barney could hear her excited chatter outside the door as Andreas came home, and his worried replies.

"Please don't be concerned," said the dark-suited man. "I am Elliott Blake, representing the firm of solicitors Frederick, Giles and Burnett. You are Barnaby Summers, I believe?"

Barney nodded, bewildered.

"I believe on two occasions you gave five pounds to a barefooted young man, for shoes."

Barney nodded again. So he HAD been tricked by a scam. He felt sad. The young man had seemed so nice.

"Yes, I thought he was homeless."

Eliott Blake laughed. "He was William de Clancy."

"Who?"

"You've not heard of him?" replied the solicitor. "He was the youngest diamond millionaire in the Western world. He has a fortune so great you could not even take it in."

"He said he had no shoes," said Barney. "I felt sorry for him."

Suddenly the phrase 'Bless you with diamonds' dell into place.

"He had no family," went on the solicitor. "He was a self-made man, and despite his wealth, he had a great social conscience. His anonymous gifts to charity were phenomenal. A while ago he was diagnosed with terminal cancer, but he refused treatment. He said he wanted to go quickly and quietly. He died two weeks ago."

Barney continued to look bewildered. What had this story to do with him, apart from the fact that he felt sorry for this kind hearted millionaire. Mr Blake smiled kindly at Barney.

"He wanted to leave his vast fortune to someone who would use it unselfishly. It seems he's been taking quite an interest in you, young man."

"Me?" cried Barney, feeling rather giddy.

"Yes, he said you had true humanity. A true love for your fellow human beings. You are his sole beneficiary."

Elliott Blake had expected Barney to be struck dumb, or to cheer, or even to burst into tears, but he was surprised and amused, when, after a moment's pause, the young man cartwheeled and then back flipped around Mrs Molly's front room.

AN INVITATION TO DINNER
Grant Bremner

The snow started just as Gary drove his Mercedes into the drive of a large Victorian mansion house, a slight tremble went through Gary's body as he parked the car. A glance at his watch informed him that he was already twenty minutes late. He briefly wondered what they might think of him for being tardy, then dismissed it, he would make a plausible excuse, he was good at that.

'Sorry to keep you waiting Gary, I was in the kitchen turning the oven down, do come in, my you are wet my dear,' remarked Olivia as she opened the front door.

'Sorry to be late, the traffic was bad due to the snow,' he lied easily wondering if she'd deliberately kept him standing out in the now heavier falling snow.

'Why don't you go and dry off, you know where the facilities are,' suggested Olivia lightly.

'Good idea,' said Gary as he headed for the downstairs bathroom.

154

'He's drying off, he'll be here in a moment,' said Olivia as she walked into the dining room.

'How does he appear?' enquired Granville gruffly.

'A little uneasy I would say, shall you pour him a drink?'

'Of course my dear, whisky and soda I believe,' said Granville as he turned to the drinks trolley. 'Your usual Olivia?'

'Thanks Granville, I'll just see to the roast, be nice when he appears.' Olivia looked Granville directly in his eyes before leaving for the kitchen.

'Ah, there you are my boy, here I've poured you a drink,' said Granville easily as Gary entered the dining room.

'Thanks for the drink,' he said as he took hold of the glass. 'Your Christmas decorations look wonderful, cheers.'

'Oh, good health my boy,' said Granville although good health was the last thing he wished for Gary.

'How's business?' Granville's tone had changed, it sounded harsh.

Gary noted the change and wasn't surprised, it was after all Granville's money that had kept the business running. 'We are doing rather well, signed a new contract only last week worth two million, so I can't complain,' answered Gary lightly, whatever happened this evening he was not going to fall out with Granville.

'Pleased to hear it my boy, although it's a great pity that Susan is not here to share in your success,' said Granville staring intently at Gary.

Gary looked at Granville wondering if he had made the correct choice in coming here this evening he could have easily made an excuse when the snow had started. Susan had died eight months ago and Gary was aware that her parents blamed him for the accident, especially as the money in her trust fund transferred to her new husband instead of reverting back to her father. However, there had been a thorough investigation by the police and no blame had been attached to him.

'I'm truly sorry that she is not here to share in the success also, I miss her you know,' said Gary with a degree of honesty. He missed Susan because she had been great at getting new clients for the business, he had just been lucky.

'Do you Gary? I heard that you have a new girlfriend, already,' remarked Olivia caustically as she appeared from the kitchen with a bowl of salad.

He was surprised that they knew about Glenda though, he'd thought that he had managed to keep her well hidden.

'Of course I miss her Olivia,' he tried to sound convincing. 'She was the world to me but life must go on and I've only had a couple of dates, my psychiatrist suggested it, help me forget the past.'

'Really, he suggested Glenda, well I guess that's modern living for you,' said Olivia sarcastically.

'No of course he didn't suggest Glenda, he said I needed to get out more see other people, that kind of thing,' retorted Gary.

'It's not even a year Gary and,' Olivia paused for dramatic effect, 'Oh dear do forgive me, we invited you for dinner as a friend and here we are about to argue, please sit and I'll bring in the roast, it's your favourite, lamb.'

'Thanks,' said Gary as he watched Olivia head off for the kitchen.

'Sorry about that Gary but you have to understand that we loved Susan very much, of course you must get on with your life, sit down my boy,' said Granville cordially.

Gary finished his drink in one go and sat down in the chair that Olivia had indicated, he was going to remain calm no matter what they said to him, he wasn't going to let them get the better of him. 'How are things with you Granville? Are you enjoying your retirement? Playing golf now?'

'No to the golf and no I am not enjoying my retirement, so things are not going so well really,' replied Granville heavily.

'Sorry to interrupt you dear, but could you do the honours?' Olivia enquired as she approached the table with the roast lamb on a silver platter.

'Of course my dear,' said Granville as he picked up the carving knife.

Gary was grateful that during dinner that there was no more mention of Susan or his new girlfriend Glenda. Granville had even opened up a couple of bottles of Château Le Gay 1990, a wine that Gary usually ordered when he was out to impress potential clients. In fact the evening had turned out much better than Gary had thought it would, all he had to do now was have a coffee then be on his way.

'You'll have a coffee Gary before you go?' enquired Olivia politely.

'That would be very nice, thank you,' replied Gary languidly as the alcohol began to take effect. 'That was a very pleasant meal Olivia, the lamb was just perfect.'

'I'm so pleased that you liked it,' said Olivia as she paused by the door. 'Granville be a dear and get Gary a nice brandy to go with his coffee.'

'I'm not sure I should Granville ...what with the wine ...I am driving,' stated Gary hesitantly.

'Just a small one then, it's only a Calvados,' said Granville as he stood up and walked towards the drinks trolley where he poured a large measure into a brandy glass.

'Can I use your bathroom?' Gary asked as he stood up from the table.

'Be my guest.' Granville watched Gary walk unevenly into the hall, then took a small phial from his breast pocket opened it and poured its content into the brandy glass.

'Here we are,' said Olivia as she walked back into the dining room. 'Is everything all right?' she enquired when she noticed that Gary was not present.

Granville beamed her a smile and held up the empty phial. 'Gary is in the toilet dear, everything is fine.'

Gary was feeling quite smug, the evening had gone much better than he'd expected. He was aware that his ex in-laws didn't care for him much, they had made that clear at the reading of Susan's will. It had come as a shock to them that Susan had made a will leaving Gary all of the money in her trust fund set up by her father. The lawyer had explained that it was perfectly legal, although he had assumed that Susan had spoken to her father about it.

Gary walked back into the dining room and took his seat. 'Most hospitable Granville, cheers,' he said before taking a hefty swig from the brandy glass.

'Down the hatch dear boy,' said Granville cheerfully as he took an envelope from his jacket pocket. 'I have something here that might interest you Gary.'

'I don't think I have time for that Granville, I have an early meeting tomorrow, I had better go,' he started to rise but somehow found he couldn't move a muscle.

Granville beamed down at him. 'Oh I think you can spare us more of your valuable time Gary, you have only a few seconds before all of your muscles seize up, anything you want to say?'

Gary began to panic, this couldn't be happening, they'd been so nice during dinner, was this a joke? 'What have you done to... 'was all he managed to say, he was completely paralysed.

Olivia walked over to where Granville was standing and looked down at Gary, she could see the fear in his eyes, the man was terrified out of his wits. 'Well done Granville.' she said cheerfully.

'Yes, it certainly worked and as quickly as I'd hoped. Want to know what I've given you Gary? Of course you do. Well it's something I've been working on these past few months, something to do in my retirement. It's a derivative of curare a neuromuscular blocking drug, paralyses the muscles almost instantly, no taste and, best of all, it metabolises quickly leaving no trace in the blood, urine or tissue.' Granville leant forwards and stared into Gary's terrified eyes.

Gary couldn't believe what he was hearing, this can't be happening to me. They were nice people, he'd liked them, he'd liked their money more but hey, what they were doing was wrong, wait, maybe they were having a joke, yes a joke, surely.'

'It's no joke Gary, just in case you were wondering, we are deadly serious,' Olivia said as she began clearing away the dinner dishes.

'This, my boy, is a report from a private detective, it makes for very interesting reading. First, he's absolutely certain that you murdered our daughter, he has enough evidence to turn over to the police to guarantee a conviction but that's not what we want, so you won't be rotting in a gaol for years.' Granville paused and looked into Gary's eyes.

'He found the bottle of Rohypnol that you thought you'd destroyed, even had your DNA on it, careless of you really Gary. The skip you threw it in, just outside your flat, had a computerised chip, apparently the council keeps a check on their movements,' said Olivia as she sat down in her chair directly across from Gary.

This can't be happening, what has that son of a bitch done to me. Jesus I can't move a bloody thing, hell's teeth they're going to kill me. Why the hell can't I move, Rohypnol doesn't do that, damn it must have been in the brandy. I scoffed the lot, please god, this can't be happening, thought Gary as he sat unable to move a single muscle.

'Look Olivia he's sweating, it's dripping down his face, pity he can't feel it, the murderer.' Granville glanced at the letter. 'You told us that Susan was going to see a friend by herself, that's why you weren't in the car with her, even said it to the police. But that wasn't true, you were with her in the car, someone saw you that night, it's taken some time only because they've been out of the country. They stopped you for directions, remember?...Aha, I see that you do.'

God the detective must have found them, he'd been worried for weeks that they might show up but they hadn't and the police finished their investigation, accident caused by alcohol, Susan had drunk too much, the coroner had said.

'They said that Susan appeared to be asleep when they spoke to you, but we know that she'd been drugged by you. You put her in the driver's seat, put the car in drive, then watched as it went over the cliff, you heartless bastard,' screamed Granville unable to control his emotions.

Gary knew now that he was a dead man, they had not gone to all of this trouble just to scare him and they'd said they weren't going to the police. He remembered that he'd felt no emotion when he'd put the tablets into Susan's drink, he had treated her death as an exercise, trying to get every part of it correct. The couple wanting directions had been traumatic, Susan might have woken up. Moving her into the driver's seat was harder than he'd imagined it would be, but then he'd been lucky as no one else approached the cliff top that evening. Please, I'm sorry, I'm really sorry, I'll let you have her money back, his eyes pleaded silently.

'I'll just take these out to the kitchen dear,' said Olivia evenly as she headed for the door.

'Right, I'll finish up in here.' Granville had regained control of his emotions. 'Now Gary, I want you to know how this will end.' He paused for a moment, his thoughts had drifted to Susan and her untimely and unwarranted death. 'It will be similar to Susan's in some respects, you will die in a car accident, but you are going to commit suicide Gary.'

Granville walked around the table and put his hand into Gary's jacket pocket and withdrew his iphone. 'Very handy these devices, what with e-mail and the like. You are going to send us one just before your drive your car into the lake, which according to the forecast might even freeze tonight. It's easier just now if I do it for you, don't you think? Oh, how remiss of me, of course you can't respond. Let's continue, you are going to say that you can't go on without Susan, Glenda was just a distraction, you felt guilty about cheating on her memory. You put on a brave face, didn't want anyone to know how much you missed her but you can't carry on without her. Olivia and I will confirm that you were very depressed, drank far too much alcohol, we even tried to get you a taxi which you adamantly refused.' Granville sat down next to Gary and opened his iphone. 'No password, how remiss of you Gary.'

Hell's teeth, why hadn't he put a password on his iphone, he'd meant to but then he was never that good in remembering passwords, Susan had been the one at work who dealt with them, so Gary could only watch as Granville typed out his suicide letter on his damned iphone.

'How's it coming dear?' Olivia asked as she pushed a wheelchair into the dining room.

Gary saw the wheelchair from the corner of his eyes and tears silently rolled down his cheeks.

'Finished, we'll take him around the back, I'll get his car, we'll dump him in it then I'll drive to the lake. I'll walk back via the golf course, it's only two miles,' said Granville.

'Wear something warm, it's freezing out and drive carefully the road may be icy in parts and don't forget to wipe the car and the iphone thoroughly,' said Olivia as she got hold of Gary's right arm.

'No, of course not, and don't you forget about the taxi,' said Granville as he took hold of the left arm.

'I won't. Merry Christmas dear.'

Gary began to scream as loud as he could, yet nobody heard him